Three Heroes, Three Decades

Coping, Loving, & Learning

Shawn Michael Nichols
Within Conflict 2025

First U.S. Edition

Edited by Barbara Bennet
Cover Design by Andjela Vujic

ISBN 13:   978-0-9994128-4-8   Paperback
ISBN 13:   978-0-9994128-5-5   eBook-Kindle

Thank You Notes

"The best paper, dissertation, or book is a finished one." I have so many people to thank who got me to this point.

My family, L, C & O, who have put up with my unique qualities with only a few eye rolls. They have influenced my perceptions and have been exceedingly patient with me over the last four years.

Dr. Mary Ann O'Neill, my friend and consult partner who was encouraging as she is fun to hang with as we giggle and put things to order.

My editor, Barbara Bennet, an editor and librarian, who I am honored to call my friend for many years.

Andjela Vujiic, a patient and talented artist who so exceeded the art I had in mind. Time zones did not keep her from doing what I never could have.

The schools, mental health institutions, and corporations that trusted me. They have truly opened my heart.

Also, C&J, Betty and Paul, Linda and Gus, Celia and Paul, and Jenn who supported me with patience, opinions, and food. What a great time you have given me.

Loving you all with great respect,

Dr. Shawn

This work and others draw on my various offerings for "The Hand" a Social Emotional Learning training tool I created to help my clients manage behavior and emotions during particularly difficult times in their lives.

This work is detailed in my book, **"Changing Habits: A Hand for Positive Transitions" 2019.**

Other Books by Shawn Michael Nichols

A Catalyst A Guardian: Brilliant Control Freaks and Strategic Micromanagers, 2017

Changing Habits: A Hand for Positive Transitions 2019

Three Heroes, Three Decades: Coping, Loving, and Learning, 2025

Three Heroes, Three Decades

Coping, Loving & Learning

Introduction – Book One

Following are three short stories, meant to be serialized, for and about teenagers. The stories are presented in chronological order to give a sense of the changing levels of sophistication each generation encounters in relation to the era: technology, availability of social media, socio-economic conditions, and national or global events.

In many cases the teens, in these short, first-in-a-series, are impacted by the issues their adults are living through. Each child is experiencing the folly of another generation's choices, without having much control themselves. Questioning who they love, and other choices may leave some of the teens with an additional layer of "life out of control."

Italicized words contained in each story are defined in the glossaries at the back of the book.

Little Stones Who Dream of Wings

A small group of young teenagers bound together by deep friendships and commitment to each other are trying to make sense of what their futures might be. In a small Midwestern town, the summer of 1976 finds the teens trying to overcome a world where being stuck and neglected are everyday problems. Their small world is shrinking further as the town itself is in decline. No one has the money to leave, and others haven't got the means to help themselves or anyone else. Yet every day that summer, they experience victories and begin to build a plan to escape together.

Renny and Jupiter

Two best friends in Stockton, circa 1993, learn to trust each other with the truth about who they are, what they want to be, and survival in Stockton, California, one of the most dangerous cities in the USA. Hindered by their family's immigrant status, the two boys, their friends, and even the crimes that may hurt them all, force changes as they must grow up far faster than their peers elsewhere. A found treasure becomes a nightmare and throws everyone in their community into distrust of each other. How do the boys find stability when even adults are failing? The young people and their teachers bear many changes and take the situation into their own hands.

Amira Ding Dong

Trying to get by among rich classmates, Amira, a struggling student must face reality. Her brother, despite being her true source of motivation and stability, will never be all he can. Racist classmates and even others who love her make her days tough. Her broken family and the wealth of others is a constant reminder that she must succeed even as she helps her friends on the verge of some terrible choices and actions.

Little Stones Who Dream of Wings

A small town in the Midwest, 1976

Introduction to Our Gang

(Definitions for words in italics can be found in the Glossary at the back of the book.)

Our little gang hangs out together almost every day, passing time at the small-town store or an abandoned housing project just outside our super quiet town. We talk about what we would buy if we had money, what the future is going to be like, and our frustrations regarding small town life. The adults in our kids' lives are doing the best they can without much money, some serious mental and emotional health issues of their own, and a strong sense, the kids share, of being passed over.

We try to be *upbeat* but sometimes things just don't work out. We haven't got much of a say, so you gotta roll with it or it drives you hard crazy every day. They say there are spirits here but hey! if the spirits can't leave, what chance do we have? Life is tough everywhere but not in Los Angeles, Hollywood, where Cascade hopes to go someday. We're all hoping to hitch a ride with her when it comes to pass. We haven't got anything to lose.

Let me tell you about our gang. First there's Ozzie whose 13. He says he's biracial. He lives with his *adopted* uncle, a local pastor, and his aunt. He's got this big, clanky tool belt and he adds lost tools to it all the time just in case something needs to be fixed. He gets a little bit of work, and he shares his small money with us. He and his family are very religious.

Mutton is super smart but quiet. She's 14 and her momma says she has an eating disorder, cause she's kind of chunky. Mutton is great. She shares her allowance with us. Whenever one of us is down low, Mutton will talk us through it.

Riley, he's a funny little guy. He's only 9 but he talks as well as us. He swears a lot, runs away a lot, and at 9 he already knows he's *ADHD, which is attention deficit – hyperactive disorder.* He's always in motion and talks constantly about searching for his real parents.

Cascade is beautiful. She's not sure if she's a 14-year-old boy or girl so she's trying both acts out. She claims she can hear the ocean waves all the time calling her to the West Coast. It helps her deal with her sadness. Though she's super smart too, she doesn't share much with us. She's super quiet.

Arlo is 12 but he talks like he's an adult. He can act funny, like odd, but when you think about it, he sees more of the future than we do.

The adults sure are mixed up but really cool at the same time. Some of us don't know who our parents are. The adults kind of boss us around but they mean good things for us.

Adria is Mutton's mom. She's way cool to us and takes us on rides to Oaks Corner. Mutton said her mom has *Munchausen by Proxy,* but I think she's always worried about Mutton and her condition. It's all Adria can talk about.

Old Mr. Johnson is the Black dude who owns the store, and he is very cool. He's probably the richest person in our town but he gets in dark moods and won't let us in the store for the rest of the day if he's feeling badly. He gives good advice too.

Old Miss Abby is Riley's foster mom. She has wild gray and red hair, loves us kids and tells us stories making us laugh. Sometimes she has straw or leaves in her hair and she's always in her garden. Sometimes, she swears a lot for no reason, but Riley says she can't help it. That's just the way she is. She and Riley take care of each other.

Olive and Juno are Cascade's moms. These two are truly the most interesting people in town. We keep an eye on them because they go real places, like faraway, D.C. and L.A. They don't care what Cascade does if she comes when she's called. They are always making plans we might be interested in. They are artists with a lot of junk in the front yard.

Old Gunther is Arlo's grandpa. He's kind of strict but he and Arlo listen to each other. Sometimes he talks likes he crazy and Arlo just takes his hand and leads him back home. Mr. Johnson says Gunther is *schizophrenic*, but he doesn't say it like it's a joke or insult. "It just is," is the way Mr. Johnson explains it.

Melanie and Gabriel Trumpet are Ozzie's adopted aunt and uncle. They run a small church in town and are always coming up with new schemes. These schemes must not work out because they're stuck with us small fish.

Our Town

"Neither this nor that." That's what people said about our small-town town of Neezer Place in Fruelein County which means: nothing in town seemed to be what it really is. This sad saying may have come from the original German settlers. Neezer Place, population 462, is served by a 60-child K-8 school, and a small food store operated by Mr. Johnson. There is also a trucker's depot with a small diner, a laundromat, and several large factories sitting empty on the edge of town. Many homes out there and in-town are abandoned or have squatters who exist on the fringes of the usual world.

These squatters are generally friendly, and the kids at least don't mind them. We wonder though if you must stop someplace; why here? We got enough problems to have to worry about, so the adults we give them a pass. It's tough.

Our high school is 36 miles away in the town of Oak Corners. Neezer residents talk about one day "having it together" and moving to Oak Corners, population 8,465. It's fun to go there and just get out of Neezer.

Chapter 1: The Tribe

I thought quiet Cascade never seemed to need us. Turns out, I was wrong about her and many other things, as I learned that summer. One day Cascade was a handsome gentle boy, then another day she was a beautiful, *introverted* girl. You'd never know what he or she would be like each day, but we welcomed her and her funny, creative clothes. She gave us hope with her fancy daydreams, acting out the soap operas and programs she had seen on TV. Later, I realized she was our *optimist*, keeping us from getting low and down. She was hella smart. Every tribe has its dreamer, and all the rest, well we just keep hoping. She had a plan early on and I think we all grabbed onto her plan because we hadn't any real strategies of our own. Adults thought we didn't have a clue just being kids, but in a small desperate town, we learned lots more than adults thought we did.

Arlo liked to argue with Cascade. He said it made them better thinkers, but I think Cascade was annoyed with him or pretended to be. Hard to tell, because if she was chatty with anyone it was Arlo. Arlo was scary smart too, and he'd never shut up. He could have been in more trouble at school for the way he talked to adults, but they cut him some slack. Most days anyway. I thought then our Arlo would change the world. I wasn't sure if he'd be working for the government, or they would be hunting for him. Still, he inspired me.

The adult folks had little money, but we still gathered in front of Mr. Johnson's tiny old store almost every late afternoon through all seasons. He didn't seem to mind when the store was empty of customers. The elderly Black man would hand out a couple of soda pops to split and then sit with us on the battered front *stoop*. Listening to our chatter, he'd offer some pretty good advice unless he was having one of his bad days. Then he'd slam the door shut, put up the closed sign, and keep us out. Adults can be touchy, but we knew this wasn't about us.

Mr. Johnson's store was at the center of our town on the one quiet road running through Neezer. Though the tiny truck stop restaurant, a quarter mile down the road, was a place where interesting things happened, interesting to us anyway, the store was the place for information, help, and gossip. I can still smell it in my mind; the sawdust, the sweet fruit and vegetables, and the sugar from all the candy placed close to Mr. Johnson to keep people from helping themselves and offering to pay another day. My mind's memory holds that particular smell close to my soul.

No school for the summer meant we had our days and evenings free. Which wasn't such a big deal as there never seemed anything to do. Each of us filled our mornings with our own "business." The rest of the time we hung together because we were almost all we had. Things were tough all around, so we avoided each other's homes unless it was a crisis. Not everyone had a phone, so we *hollered* from the street to the front door. We gave each other space and I think this allowed everyone some personal dignity. Dignity and privacy were important to us kids.

Being in our small tribe kept us safe. Safe from older kids, maybe from our homes too, and the adults around us. We knew stuff about each other, and this also brought us together. We needed to belong to something. We looked after each other.

What did I know then? Not much.

Riley was 9 and swore more than any adult we knew. Funny and twitchy, our townsfolk said, Riley was the engine in our small troop. He'd plant this grimace on his face until you'd finish with your story and then he'd go trying to solve it or explain it. When you're nine, you think you're superman.

Mutton, the other girl in our pack, and her mom made our gossip almost every day. Mutton, nick-named so by her mom, shared her snack money with us, allowing each one to pick out something. We were grateful for her and her mother's generosity. Her snack money also kept us in good graces with Mr. Johnson who could *abide* customers but not *parasites*. He claimed our town was filled with troublemakers, slackers, and parasites. Then he'd smack the counter or wooden stoop with his big flat palm in *exasperation*.

Mutton was a blonde heavy girl, light on her feet, taller than the boys, and was a friend to everyone, speaking well of and supporting the underdogs of our small town. Cascade would arrange Mutton's hair, using her own hairclips as they talked more intimately, whispering together at times.

Mutton seriously considered everything she was told and often didn't respond to the conversations right away. When she did however, she was the one who set us all right, in a good way. Her *musings* kept us thinking for days and in this way, we'd pick up conversations on and off for months.

Our town was a funny place in an odd state. The summers were so hot, the day took your breath away, and the winters so bitterly cold, you froze to your core. You could walk the main street in ten minutes, and the whole town in about twenty. We all wore our proud shoes, the ones you'd let your friends see and each pair carried us around most for the year, summer, and winter. *Civilization* as we knew it was a car ride away and no buses ran through this part of the county.

Adria took her daughter, Mutton, on regular visits to Oak Corners to see her two dads and to health clinics for her weight. Adria was almost always sunburned though quite pretty, maybe too thin, and dressed in thrift store hand-me-downs like the rest of us. Mutton declared her mom had a flair unlike the rest of us. Adria gave us rides in her old sunburnt '67 Eldorado when she ran errands. *The 8-track player* was broken but we could listen to any radio station we wanted. At times we sang along, though Adria might stop us if she had one of her headaches.

Just about everyone one in our town wore some type of hand me down. I think back now how we struggled to make these clothes acceptable and even give us some dignity. My friends dressed for our time together. We wanted to fit in, but we admired the clothing changes we each tried to make. When you're young, your appearance is both your armor and your weak spot.

Remember funny, serious Ozzie? Ozzie told us we were all going to see Satan one day, but he agreed with a *philosophical* shrug he'd probably be there with us. "Everyone's a sinner," Ozzie said, unless you have money and then you could make yourself okay by contributing to the Lord's work. "It was all over television" he argued with conviction, and Cascade confirmed this by describing the clothes

15

and elaborate stage sets or churches the TV *televangelists* had. This style thing was a shared mystery for them, though they explicitly disagreed on religious matters.

Only Ozzie went to church, though he never bugged us about going along. Quietly chewing on the inside of his mouth most of the time, with a good word of warning now and then, Ozzie would slide away when his Aunt Melanie and uncle, Pastor Gabriel Trumpet roared up in their Oldsmobile station wagon with the fake wood paneling, They'd find us at the store or Tropical Acres, the unfinished, decaying housing development we hung out in along with all the other kids from Neezer Place.

Tropical Acres was our playground, clubhouse, and safe hideout. Just outside town, the abandoned housing project could not have been a better playground. Every group of kids and teenagers claimed a house or space and we left each other alone. Kids can find their space among others and leave each other in peace if you let them.

I thought then we'd know each other, one way or the other, always.

Chapter 2: Riley's Gone

"He's gone Mr. Johnson, my lil' boy is gone, and I don't know what to do. I try to love him the best I can, but he's angry hurt to find his real mommy and daddy. He left before I was even up today."

Abby, Riley's foster mom, was at the store that afternoon. Distraught, nervous, and shaking, Abby allowed Mr. Johnson to comfort her. She swigged from a bottle of orange soda he had gently placed in her hand without her fully realizing it, and now she was gasping between gulps.

Mr. Johnson knew Abby stayed up all night watching late night cable television and buying rip-off products using her state money, and often, forgetting to pay her rent. Because of this she roused herself late in the morning, or even afternoon if it was too hot outside, and then set about taking care of Riley and her beautiful, wonderful, overgrown garden.

Abby's garden was truly one of the few wonders of the town. She could put anything into the ground and soon the colorful and varied plants grew above the fence and some even near to the roof of the house or shed. This was a time before other people talked to growing things but somehow it helped her cope with her condition. The fruits and vegetables were the best you ever tasted. A generous woman to everyone in town she would place small groupings of her garden's bounty on the neighbor's porches for them to enjoy later.

School days, Abby would show up at our playground with a small sad lunch for Riley, lovingly made and packed. Sometimes, it was a can of sardines and a bun, and other day's some fresh fruit and saltines. She'd bring a huge bouquet of flowers or a bag of sweet fruit from her famous garden to give to all the teachers and humbly request, please, would they look after her small eccentric boy, little Riley.

In conference with the teachers, Abby ducked her head *acknowledging* the small boy could be hard to handle, physically, and emotionally. He was special, she proudly informed them. Riley's teachers did the best they could to reassure Abby and manage her small charge. These weekly conferences consisted of the teachers doing all the talking and Abby bobbing her head with an agreeable, hopeful smile on her chubby face. She'd take her knotted headscarf off her head and either fan her face or wipe the sweat from her brow as the meeting droned on. These gentle talks were *difficult* for her and as the teachers expected, she immediately forgot all the negative things the teachers said. Later she'd proudly tell Riley, how the teachers were constantly praising him.

Several years earlier, Abby had accepted the mostly-rural state's offer of a foster child to increase her *medical support payments*. Children Riley's age did not often get taken up quickly for adoption and Riley himself had made the few *potential* parents uncomfortable enough to look elsewhere. He was as Abby said, determined to find his REAL parents. These searches usually came to involve the whole town and though most grew tired of the little kid's behavior, many were anxious to help his tiny, sweet soul.

The social worker, Miss Wentworth, and some of our gang had gently explained to Riley he might be better off here with Abby. Riley considered this

18

carefully each time but, in the end, decided if this were true, he could be of some help to his real parents. "Who knew what danger they might be in?" the nine-year old boy asked himself.

We knew and understood many parents did not stay together after giving up a child for adoption. Riley fantasized his father was some wealthy married guy who'd had ruined a young girl's life. This was something Riley and Cascade had seen in soap operas. In time, Riley settled on this story which only made him more anxious to find her or them and help them. In either case, Riley had to go and go now. He was NEEDED!

"Mr. Johnson, what will I do? He's the best little boy and you know some days he's the one taking care of me. I get my spells and shakes, and Riley, sweet kid, he just tries to make me laugh and get normal again. He brushes my hair every day." A long sob escaped Abby's mouth and open mouthed, she belched heartily. The tears started dripping down her face and from her chin *unimpeded*. Mr. Johnson handed her a paper towel which she ignored, wiping her tears across her face and into her long shaggy gray hair with the back of her solid, wrinkled hand. Her *Goodwill* barber's jacket which identified her as Fred, was *askew* and a bit dirty at the cuffs. Her grey work pants, frayed and mended, were too long and sagged around her battered wooden *clogs*.

"Now, Miss Abby, Riley's done this before, and he never gets very far. All the troopers know him by now and we don't get many visitors through Neezer," Mr. Johnson intoned quietly but with authority. "He's probably asleep somewhere,

19

tired from a long walk and he'll be hungry and head back home. You should try to be calm and not frighten him when he returns."

"Has the social worker told you about his situation?" Mr. Johnson asked thinking aloud. "You and I both know not to open any doors to the past, but this little guy seems like he could use some information to brighten his day. Not sure saying they died, but if they have, it might calm him though. Have you told him he can search when he's sixteen? Maybe tell him to make himself better at school, find a job, and have some money when he really starts to look?" Mr. Johnson was an *emphatic* philosopher and *determined* fixer.

Abby looked at Mr. Johnson with hurt in her watery eyes. "He's my boy, Mr. Johnson. Whoever they WERE, they have not looked for him. And I'm glad. He's MY boy!" She continued to slurp the empty bottle hoping Mr. Johnson would stand her another soda but he was *disinclined* to be that generous. This Riley matter happened often and *inevitably*; Abby came to him.

The first time Riley had taken a long, almost one-way walk, she had called the troopers and the social worker, and the event had not gone at all well. Really badly in fact. Abby had been upset and *hysterical* and the then *retrieved* six-year-old Riley tried to lead her back in the house so the assembled neighbors would not laugh at her. In the end, the social worker decided Riley would be as much trouble in another home, but Abby would totally fall apart if her *determined* little boy was gone. He was only five when he came to her and he had sorted, in her view, her life out. Taking care of Abby was a lot to put upon a small *resolute* child but it kept him busy.

20

By now, us kids were all assembled in a straight row in front of Miss Abby, knowing Riley would return, but supporting Miss Abby the only way we knew how. There was always the chance Mr. Johnson would reward us for our support with a couple of Twinkies. Picture several rattily dressed kids standing in a row witnessing and nodding our heads together as Mr. Johnson shared his common sense. We were almost 80% sure he would come back. Well 70% anyway. We'd seen tv shows about kids out alone, and though these stories kept us close to town, we could not deny it was always exciting when someone else chanced it. We'd love and smother Riley with hugs when he returned. Riley was just so brave we had decided so long ago.

"Riley's smart and just because he's small doesn't mean he can't take care of himself, Miss Abby," Mutton declared. "Look how much experience he has at this, right guys? I mean I couldn't do this even once and get back here safe, you know? I need my mom so much; I'd never try it though." Miss Abby started crying again thinking Riley didn't need her after all. Maybe she was too much of a burden for him. Miss Abby *blubbered* even louder.

"God will take care of him, Miss Abby." Ozzie tried to soothe the distraught woman. "Our Lord is there for everyone, especially children and animals. It says so in the Bible, Book of Matthew." Ozzie was sincere and he held his hand over his heart as he had been taught. He also knew how to use his counseling voice which almost always made us cry and change our minds about what evil we had been intent on committing. Sometimes sharing a problem with Ozzie could be a pain.

"Yeah, Ozzie. What's the part about suffer the little children…? Something about that in the Bible, isn't there? It means the children will have to die to come to Jesus, Fart Head!" Though friends, smart Arlo could not resist a challenge to Ozzie's calm and seemingly *self-assured* posture.

Miss Abby started crying again and slid, backside down the front of the counter with her legs *akimbo*. Mr. Johnson rolled his eyes and not for the first time when we or Miss Abby were around.

Mr. Johnson shrugged, at first uncertain what to do, picked up his battered *beige* office phone off the shelf behind him and dialed the troopers. He was anxious himself about the little boy, but he needed us all out of the store before this new problem began to affect him. Stress seemed to kick him harder than most people. He could fake it for a bit but when things got loud or out of control his mind began to wander, and strange pictures flashed in front of his eyes. Pretty soon, he'd be imagining the young boy in some dangerous setting, and he would turn himself into a fearful, angry Black version of the Hulk. This transformation had been a terrible thing in his past, he *grimaced*. "Concentrate," Mr. Johnson said over and over in his inner mind. This isn't like that time when he was twelve. This was easier.

Arlo walked around the counter and put his arm upon Mr. Johnson's hunched back. To our surprise, the old man did not reprimand or push Arlo away. Arlo lightly rubbed Mr. Johnson's back in small circles, and it seemed to make the man quiet and purposeful. He wasn't getting chased by the speeding truck filled with laughing, screaming white men, Mr. Johnson reminded himself.

22

He spoke shortly and swiftly to the operator who promised to place an alert to the county troopers. The operator would also place a call herself to Oak Corners' Police Department just in case Riley had or would get so far away. Unlikely, though there was a lot of quiet ground around between here and there and badgers were spotted all the time.

Badgers were everywhere in our county, and maybe some scary black bears too. One hot afternoon as we *lazed* in our favorite broken down house in Tropical Acres, Mutton had whistled low to us. Just off the broken concrete patio a mother badger and her twin babies *rummaged* in the long weeds, snorting, and looking for anything not fried by the strong sunshine. The badger looked like a low flat dog, part turtle and part bear we had decided. It waddled now but could move swiftly, faster than any of us, if it decided to protect its babies.

We all stayed quiet, unmoving, watching it, half-excited as it moved just below us a few feet away. Cascade said she'd been in a trance from the heat, only realizing later how much danger we were in. The animal smelled horrible. Why hadn't we smelled it? Arlo explained the animal was downwind of us, so we wouldn't catch the *stench*, but it should have been more wary as it must have smelled our lot. Arlo guessed the badger was used to smelling us in a particular place. It was our house and maybe her house too. Our house away from home and adults.

Kids and tramps had claimed the two dozen or so uncompleted, now *decrepit* houses in this overgrown abandoned area. No one remembered the developer who'd spent his *inheritance* building the place as a second-home-community for overworked, and relatively *well-to-do* downstate people who would come north for a break and some skiing. No one bought here as the land for hundreds of miles in all directions was perfectly flat. Add in badgers and bears in the summertime and it wasn't such a tropical paradise after all.

Arlo would add adults were so bad at planning if their mind was only on money. We didn't want to live here, why would anyone else?!? Still, it was a great hangout even on rainy days. In the winter, we'd build a fire on the concrete foundation like the older kids and homeless people did in their house *squats*.

"Hey kids," Mr. Johnson surprised us out of our reverie. "Do you think you could walk Miss Abby home and fix her up a bit? She needs to calm down before the troopers show up with Riley, AS I'M SURE HE WILL, right kids? Just a short trip for our brave little guy, right?" Mr. Johnson's eyes grew wide and unblinking whenever he tried to make a point of getting us to do something.

We nodded together, having performed this act many times before. Cascade pulled two purple butterfly clips out of her long blonde hair and used them to push Miss Abby's gray hair back over her ears. This made her look a bit silly and we giggled as we started our rescue mission. We all grabbed a leg or an arm and tried to get the older lady on her feet.

"1, 2, 3, oof!" With the last push Miss Abby assisted our efforts and though unsteady on her feet, we could direct her with her own *locomotion*. Down the front steps of the store and out into the sunshine we headed back to Riley's foster home like a small parade of warriors with their dazed prisoner, butterflies clinging to the side of her head.

Riley returned much later and only Ozzie was left in the house with Miss Abby by then. Ozzie had been chatting and praying, as Miss Abby watched television and paced worriedly to and from her front window concerned this time, Riley might not be so lucky. She suppressed this thought by squeezing her eyes so hard it made her head pound.

Everything in life seemed to give her a headache. Abby had been having them for as long as she could remember. The doctors explained to her perhaps early in her young life, she'd probably *sustained* some damage from a fall or blow from something heavy. On certain days when she felt clear in her head, and could manage it, pictures showed up in her brain. Pictures of family, some good and some bad, and she'd be struck by a powerful feeling of happiness mixed with sadness and fear. Not all bad, though some pictures scared her so much, it was a good thing she didn't recognize people or herself in these brain images.

The busy crickets and grasshoppers were singing in a high chorus under a full moon by the time Riley returned. As the young local officers knocked on the door, Miss Abby collapsed into her old cotton-floral covered chair, afraid of the news. She frantically motioned Ozzie to the door, who ran head-on into Riley as he came in the unlocked door. The *contrite* little boy was intent on wrapping his short, sunburned arms around his foster mother and reassuring her, even as he shoved his own disappointment down into his gut. He had failed again at finding his parents. He hadn't gotten any further than before and now Miss Abby might be in trouble.

The troopers, a young man and woman known to the townsfolk, aware of Miss Abby's usual condition treated her well, and only asked if they could get her or Riley anything. She hugged them both and foggily gave each one a battered can of soup as a reward, which they *graciously declined*. For the rest of the evening, Riley and Abby watched television together until long after midnight, packed tight in her chair together without speaking much.

The kind troopers gave a still-calm Ozzie a ride home and when his aunt and uncle came out, anxious about the day, the officers gave the couple a description of what they had seen.

Driving up a rarely-used side road, they saw a very small figure lying on the cracked *asphalt*. Not really lying so much as keening in a rigid posture, with his feet and shoulders planted on the ground and his mid-section raised in the air; his arms clamped hard at his sides. His screams and motions scared the officers, uncertain of the little man's mental health. They approached quickly and cautiously and the small child, Riley as it turned out, began to calm down when they spoke to him. They'd never seen anything like it. What was it called?

Ozzie's aunt and uncle shrugged and sighed. They saw many instances of devil *possession* in these poverty-stricken parts. These *afflictions* came and went, they confessed. Would the officers like to take some *brochures* about their bingo nights and prayer vigils? The officers declined these gifts too.

During these events, we were confused by our love for Riley and our fears for his safety. We cheered him like a hero but couldn't come to terms easily with the risks he took so often. What was each one of us going to have to do to make something change in our *environment*? No one could really walk so far and where would we end up?

A few days later, on a bright afternoon when pink furry clouds were running across the sky with the wind, Mr. Johnson questioned Riley about what came over him when he ran away. What was he thinking? Did he feel different? Was he panicky?

Riley in a somber mood, *melancholy* but calm now, told the older man his own story of panic, fear, and the need to run. Just run. "I love Abby and she loves me, but I don't belong here. Not with you or any of you." By now, we were beginning to join Mr. Johnson and the small boy on the store's front steps. "I just get crazy," Riley confessed, "and I don't know why." His small shoulders, in a faded red shirt, held a long shrug to match his wandering mind. He stared far away from us, his small *monotone* voice.

Mr. Johnson thoughtfully patted him on the shoulder and told Riley he was a brave boy and he too, Mr. Johnson, had his moments. Tough, angry, scared moments when he did not know what to do. We *contemplated* the man and boy, knowing this already, because we had witnessed both young boy and old man in the *descent* of their despair. These spells made all of us *hypervigilant* when we sensed something was starting to go wrong with either one. How could we protect them if the adults were unable to help?

"Listen, Riley. I once spent some time in a place where they tried to help me. I lived there for a time, helped run the place, cooking and cleaning, but went to meetings all day long. There was this very old white guy. Looked like the old white

27

guy who sells chicken in a bucket on TV. He said some interesting things. Most of the time we messed around, with these smug speakers. They didn't know us or our experiences. How could they help us? This guy he was okay. He liked us, respected us, and told us we were brave. He gave us a method to cheat on anger and nervousness. Those words got us listening. Cheating? We thought we knew everything in those days about cheating people. Sometimes though, you just need another way to calm yourself down, right?"

Mr. Johnson held up his long, *elegant* thumb, with well-groomed nails. "Come on watch me and do it too," he asked. He glared at us to join in, one eyebrow cocked.

"This is your thumb but it also represents you. Everything about you; your thoughts, your past, your future, your emotions, and what makes you, you." We all held our thumbs up and repeated after the man.

"This is your thumb but it's also you. Everything about you; your thoughts, your past, your future, your emotions, and what makes you, you" we all whispered dutifully.

"This is your index finger. It is all the **good and bad** that comes to you in your life. It's ice cream and hunger, friends, and bullies, freezing nights and hot summer days. It makes you feel some emotion inside."

"This is your index finger. It is all the good and bad that comes to you in your life. It's ice cream and hunger, friends, and bullies, freezing nights and hot summer days. It makes you feel something inside" glancing sideways we continued checking on other's progress helpfully.

This is your middle finger. It's all about emotions coming from these visitors." Mutton giggled and Ozzie pulled a grim face but followed along. "Yes, right. We use this finger when we are angry, but in our anger, there is joy, sadness, and hopefully some love and joy. Emotions are mixed up because we are learning, some days our best friend is our worst enemy." At this point, Mr. Johnson became silent and let out a long sigh thinking of the friend who had put him away for some time. The person he had trusted with his money and secrets.

"Yes, sometimes, people and things are not what we think."

We repeated the whole thing mumbling badly, shrugging at each other. "This is your ring finger. It is a reaction or no action resulting from your emotions. Reactions can be a hurtful word or a hug, a smile or sneer, a pat on the back or screaming in your face. What we do about emotions, the old guy said, changes everything in our world. We must learn to control our reactions to save ourselves and get people to really see us."

Again, we rambled through the man's words until we just drifted back to silence. Shrugs again.

"Your pinkie finger is the consequences of your actions and reactions. Some are good and some are bad. We don't think about *consequences* while we're acting in happiness or rage. We just don't see it coming." He paused.

We were silent waiting for the next bit, but Mr. Johnson eyes became watery and as he stood up, he emphatically promised to finish *anger management* using *The Hand*© for us later.

29

Chapter 3: Cascade Takes a Ride

"She was all dressed up in her *harem outfit*, hanging onto a ratty suitcase, and about ready to get into a truck! That trucker was smiling like he'd won the Kentucky Derby or something! Walking dainty; everyone in the parking lot standing and watching her without doing a dang thing. What is going on with your girl?!" Gunther gestured to Cascade standing *contritely* beside her moms with a battered pink suitcase at her feet.

Gunther, Arlo's grandpa was so angry, he was shaking. The towering man with long gray hair wearing an *immaculately* pressed shirt and *khaki* pants, was spitting as he explained what almost happened to Cascade's for her two moms, Olive, and Juno, to understand. Was he getting through to them?

"I mean what, what was she going to do when AND IF she made it to Los Angeles, or Beverly Hills, or some bad house in Las Vegas! I do my best to keep Arlo in place without too much trouble, and you all know it's not easy for me. Don't you two care? Too busy with your hippie art life so you can't take an Almighty minute to check on your kid," Gunther heatedly *petitioned* the two 30-something women, their arms crossed, heads cocked to the side. He took a folded brilliant-white handkerchief from his pants pocket and wiped at the sweat pouring down his forehead and neck.

The two women gave him a hard look right back, their eyes narrowed. Olive was from the south, a Black woman with two *advanced degrees* and lots of world *sophistication*. She'd had plenty of white men shouting at her in her life, especially after her move north, and she wasn't going to take it from one more

30

claiming she was an unfit mother. She uncrossed and recrossed her arms; wooden bracelets clanking and threw back her head.

"Listen old man, we are grateful for what you did. It's true we are busy, but we don't have to explain this to you or any other man. Cascade, like every child in the world is going to take chances. Women must because you and your type have made it so. This moment was unfortunate and thanks to you it ends well. We will discuss it with Cascade and come to an understanding. Now leave us alone. And yes, thank you!" Olive grabbed Cascade's suitcase and gestured for Juno and Cascade to follow her.

Juno, hesitating, appeared a little *embarrassed*. She was a local by birth, a white woman, with a high school diploma, in a mostly white state. In her childhood she knew Gunther and befriended his daughter, Arlo's mother, before she disappeared. Her unexpected departure left Arlo to Gunther. Juno and Olive had great affection for Arlo due to his respectful and loving relationship with their *trans daughter*, Cascade. Not everyone in town was so supportive.

"Gunther, thank you. I truly appreciate what you've done for us. In many ways, this town raises their kids together and Arlo and Cascade are better off for each other." She moved to hug the old man but stepped back when he grimaced.

"Olive fears this place, Gunther, and she stays for me and Cascade. I think you understand. We have a lot to do to keep our family fed and housed safely. And oh! The first summer festival went well, and we've sold a lot of the art and a ton of the jewelry." She smiled brightly, mistakenly thinking Gunther would be happy for her. Juno spent the long cold winters making costume jewelry, and

31

Olive carved and painted beautiful wood bracelets. They sold these at traveling and county fairs across the state throughout the summer, the three living in the small camper attached to their van.

Gunther looked past her at the spray-painted junk in their large front yard. The back yard was worse. He disapproved of their standards. The two women built and welded what they called "found art." Americana-style art was selling well so near the *bicentennial* and he hoped it meant the red, white, and blue junk would be gone soon. He had a hard time maintaining his own appearance when he ran out of *medications* and had to wait for the next month. But dang if he was going to let his appearance, home, or grandson slip into *decrepitude.*

"Mr. Gunther, thank you." Cascade had slipped up behind Juno, wrapping her arms around her mother's waist. "Sometimes, we all get a little crazy, you know." She smiled at him, and Gunther grimaced but nodded knowing everyone had problems. He half waved and turned back to his pickup truck. Waving again from the driver's seat, he stomped the engine to life, and spun the truck around the dirt driveway, heading back to his own well-managed home.

The three women waved him off. And later...

"Daughter, I'll show you what we made today," Olive brushed Cascade's hair before bedtime, wishing all their lives were easier. "if you tell me what brought you to such a place and *behavior* today. What were you thinking? How would you get along without us?" Cascade curled up in her mom's lap, listening to the loving woman's heartbeat.

"I wish I could tell her," Cascade thought inwardly. "How can we be so proud of our parents and then be so ashamed or angry at them? Love hurts. Do other kids love and hate their parents at the same time? This is hard," she thought. "I can't figure myself out yet and my moms are too busy with work and political marches and rallies. Someday I'll be gone. I know I'm not going to miss a thing here except them." Her mother released her and guided her to bed.

"Arlo's okay." She continued in her own mind. "He's funny and he makes me want to be smarter. I wish all people were like him," she thought sadly, as she scooted under the handmade quilts on her too-small bed. The headboard was a found object, an old wooden sign. A flat piece of plywood, faded and peeling paint, cut to be a *majorette's* smiling helmeted-head and upraised arm with a baton. Cascade had wanted it so badly when they found it years ago. Her moms had *relented*, packing into the van, and brought it home for her. It was another dusty year before they repainted it for Cascade's bed. By then, Cascade, was uninterested though fixing the headboard made her moms happy and they laughed and giggled as they worked on it. For such a moment, she started to love the artsy headboard again.

That night, the lashing summer rain, thunder, and lightning woke the entire town. These storms were vivid and those who woke sat in bedclothes at the window watching the powerful show. People who were already suffering serious illnesses were unnerved by heavy storms, frightened and edgy. Tons of rain would make the morning fresh but by afternoon the asphalt and gardens would make the air steamy and still.

Early the next morning under still hot gray skies, Cascade made her own breakfast; a hard-boiled egg, plus a piece of toast with cheese, and crawled back into an overly warm bed gingerly balancing the chipped plate. Her moms were still asleep from another long late-night discussion about Cascade, their art business, and a strong desire to leave Neezer Place behind them. Was Cascade right? Would they ever have a life here, barely paying bills, just keeping the house together, board by board? Face to face now, they snored loud and deeply into their pillows, unaware Cascade's attempt to leave had caught the attention of certain troublesome people.

Chapter 4: Gunther and his Daughter

Days later, Arlo came home from a full afternoon with his friends at the abandoned housing park. They had discussed whether they should all buy a car together or purchase bus tickets when they left Neezer Place. The group was divided on future business and whether they were all heading to the same place. Arlo was surprised his closest friends were thinking of going solo and this worried him. They had to stick together always. This was his new worry for the day. He'd add separation to a growing list of worries.

His grandfather was not yet up, and Arlo was careful not to wake the old man. He made his own dinner of pretzels, torn baloney slices perched on crackers, and slathered with huge dabs of low-fat off-brand mayonnaise. The boy sat on the worn velvet sofa, legs crossed, feeding himself, food laid on a newspaper on the sofa next to him. Often, he'd jump up to change to any of the other four TV channels for something interesting to watch. Laughing too loudly at something he saw; Arlo covered his mouth, worried about waking Gunther who would be in a wild state without his medications.

The television was turned low and unusually Gunther did not come out to check on Arlo or eat something himself. These spells occurred close to the end of the month when money and medicine were sparse. Arlo put himself to bed around midnight after looking in on his grandfather huddled in his bed facing the wall. All's well, Arlo thought.

Because of that difficult day and night, many things in our small town began to change rapidly in ways we could not control. Uncertain if these events were good or bad, or just horrible, we reacted from our young hearts and minds. We did not understand everything but, when possible, we gathered and drew even closer together.

Social services stepped in immediately to get Arlo into a good home in town if they could. It was unlikely there'd be an adoption for a boy Arlo's age, and it seemed possible the boy would be sent to a teens' foster home in one of the poor cities scattered around the state making their money in such enterprises. In the short term at least, Juno and Olive had come through and Arlo moved in with them and Cascade until decisions could be made.

As a result of the social agency's search and long *tentacles* in the matter of missing persons, the agency found Arlo's mom's last address. They sent her an official letter and in just a week, Arlo received a letter addressed to Arlo, General Delivery, Neezer Place. The curious and helpful post mistress closed the post office early and officially walked the letter over to Juno and Olive's home, where Arlo was living temporarily and yet uncomfortably.

Due to Gunther's unexpected death, Arlo was in a state of extreme grief and mourning and so it became incredibly *awkward* in the small house for everyone. He could not have stayed alone in his grandfather's house without Gunther for Arlo was having attacks of rage. Again, the world had denied him happiness in one way or another. His crying and anger were affecting the three women and one or two sculptures in the garden had suffered from Arlo's hysterical use of a mallet.

The letter read:

Dear Sweet Arlo, I am so sad to tell you baby, your mom passed away several months ago. She was my best friend and roommate, and I never knew anyone so sweet and kind. We have been like sisters, and she talked about you constantly.

You were her little man and the reason for her whole being. On her best days she swore she'd make you happy and successful. She was always trying to get some big money together to bring you out here, but work is work and a girl must make a living. Right?

She was proud to send you a few bucks each week and we both hoped it would help you understand how much she loved you but couldn't manage everything. The police took all her things in the search and if they return her photos and belongings, I will forward them onto you.

I couldn't tell you sooner as I wasn't in a good place. Good Luck in this world, right?

Best wishes, dear sweet kid. She was an incredibly good person and I hope you always know and remember.

Annabelle – Los Angeles

Arlo pondered the letter over and over. The letter was passed around the gang, and all read it aloud repeatedly and tried to comfort the boy. The reference to money being sent each week kept popping up like a noisy bird late at night, crying, "pay attention to me" in all their heads. Gunther had never mentioned receiving anything from his mother and even if money had been sent, Arlo was sure his grandfather would have told him. Gunther would have used the funds to care for them both. It was only right. Still, there were some nagging thoughts and Arlo shared all these with his friends, including Mr. Johnson.

Philosophical Ozzie, with some compassion, foresaw "Arlo's mom waiting for a hitchhiker's ride to hell with her friends along the way." Mutton gave Ozzie a cold eye and warned him to shut his mouth.

Riley saddened, yet *intrigued*, demanded to know if Arlo's mom had been in Hollywood. If so, it wasn't such good news for the gang and Cascade made no reference to her long-awaited destination. Cascade told herself she had to be more careful and not simply jump when she felt like it. Good to know! She'd write the warning down in her diary!

It was Mutton who suggested, "Arlo, if your mom sent money, Gunther wouldn't have used it unless it was an emergency. Arlo, he loved you! Where would he put the money if he didn't put it in the bank? Have you checked the bank in Oak Corners?"

They settled down in a circle on the dried-out lawn, each becoming thoughtful, each twisting the problem into a riddle to be solved. After a few minutes of quiet, Ozzie, finger pointed upward for effect, commanding Mutton and the rest of our gang, " I have the tools. Let's go look!"

Chapter 5: Ozzie Has It Out

Melanie hummed as she put the tv dinners with their hot foil containers down on the small green card table in Pastor Gabriel's jumbled office. She placed a few paper napkins in the center of the table and asked Ozzie to bring the water jug and jelly glasses they used for beverages from the cabinet in the small closet.

"Yes, ma'am." The young boy jumped up from the worn blue sofa closing his personal bible and carefully bending the page corner to save his place to read later before lights out.

"Son! I've told you it is disrespectful to treat the Bible of Our Lord and God in such a manner. Haven't I?" Pastor Gabriel belched his judgement on the young boy as the thin bony balding man continued to read the local newspapers from the towns around. Many a good opportunity in the For Sale, Lonely Hearts, and Free-To-A-Good-Home sections of the paper, the Pastor mused.

"Yes, Sir." The truth was Ozzie read his precious Bible over and over. It was his dearest and most important possession besides his tool belt. He claimed he cared for no other objects in his life, speaking with such conviction he surprised even his young friends. The Bible was the first thing he remembered receiving which was truly his. It was a part of him now. The tool belt became an obsession and Ozzie would pick up old tools around town as neighbors would leave them out for him. His collection extended beyond his belt and into a shoebox where he kept the tools he retired but never *relinquished*.

"Interesting thing, Ozzie, you helping Arlo find his granddad's stash his poor troubled mother had been sending him all these years. If you knew about it, you might have told us first. We are your *guardians* and not so sure we don't deserve some of the money." The man licked his lips at the thought of so much unreported cash coming into his pockets.

"Why Ozzie, it might even have got you into a good Christian college," cooed Aunt Melanie. "You could have been our best bet yet. I mean the state money doesn't even begin to cover the expense of raising you and training the devil out of you. You and this whole town know we have loved you as our own from the day they placed your scared little two-year-old self in our care. Not a finer family to grow up with in this God-forsaken town. I hope you know this, and appreciate our sacrifice, son." Melanie placed her hand upon Ozzie's forearm, part of the training they all had received to truly touch people when counseling them.

She ruffled Ozzie's bushy, uncut Afro, bending down to smell it deeply, then satisfied, plumped herself down on one of the chairs from a free-to-a-good-home donation. "Don't forget to shower tonight, Ozzie. You know how sweaty you get, and God does not abide a sloppy soul. Does he, Pastor?"

The thin man with yellowed teeth gazed over at his still *glamourous, curvaceous* young wife. He never understood her complete faith in him all these years. She could have done better even around here. She was the one who suggested they foster young kids and at times they'd had a few in the back rooms of the *sanctuary*. The state had basic payments for such situations, and the money though good, was never enough.

41

Melanie, sweet soul, truly loved each kid passing through their office/home and went through dark spells over kids she'd only known for a short time after they left. Her love made a difference in their lives, and they *flourished* in her care. Melanie had the ability to make each child feel competent and loved. She asked them to raise their own awareness of their special importance within the small fragile family group she provided. She was grateful to receive the cards from her foster children from around the Midwest.

"No Sir, the Lord does not like a sloppy soul in a body provided by His Grace." Melanie *smirked* at the Pastor's words and Ozzie ignored the Pastor's remarks in view of the man's *ill-kempt* appearance. "Well, let's see how Arlo and the state decide to share the money. I may have to speak with a lawyer, right, my lovely little wife?"

Melanie and Ozzie abruptly stopped eating their still-frozen-at-the-center tv dinners and stared neutrally at the Pastor. He glanced up, surprised to receive such unusually complete attention. "I'm not saying we are entitled to a share of the money, but a good Christian would consider the helpfulness of our young son here, in initiating the search. I mean, it's the right thing to do." They settled back into eating, all with their own new uncomfortable concerns.

The rest of dinner passed quietly, but Ozzie was troubled about the pastor's *venal* intentions. Arlo was his friend despite being a future citizen of hell notwithstanding Ozzie's best efforts. As was his style, Ozzie would think upon this new problem and prepare a sermon about the subject. He might even deliver this one. He'd been writing the Pastor's sermons for almost a year now and shaking up some people, his uncle said. His uncle never gave him credit publicly, but Aunt Melanie was supportive and explained to Ozzie how a good team worked. Each to his highest talent.

The next day,

Arlo was at the Oak Corners bank with Mr. Johnson and Ms. Juno at his side. They all explained the situation about Gunther and the miraculous find. They all agreed, including the Bank Manager, the money should be moved to a safe place. The Manager had searched the bank's records and files. Attached to a small checking account with several hundred dollars in it, Gunther had placed Arlo's full name as the beneficiary of his estate, including the house.

The mention of the house surprised all of them. There appeared to be no mortgage on the 80-year-old house. It was free and clear, though the bank's lawyers would make certain of in the next week.

The manager advised the group they would allow small withdrawals against the account until it was determined there were no other heirs or expenses existing on the house or money. That day, Arlo held back a little cash with the intention of giving his grandad a party send off with food and lemonade for his friends and neighbors.

Chapter 6: Mutton's secrets are revealed, and her mother goes to Oak Corners. Ozzie uses his tools.

Mutton stared *balefully* into the mirror, pushing her long blonde hair back behind her ears, turning and twisting her face this way and that hoping to see some of the beauty she saw in other girls. She picked up her brush and pulled it slowly through her hair now, counting out the strokes making it shine and glow.

She knew inside she was a beautiful person; for the things she loved, for the people she cherished, and even her steady approach to her small world made her certainly worthwhile. Her peaceful acceptance of who she was, was fragile due to her mother's approach to parenting. Adria, her mother, constantly bad-mouthed Mutton's eating habits; insulting her when she thought Mutton was overindulging. But dang! it was difficult. Her mother bought her all sorts of cupcakes and candy bars because, as Adria said, "Mutton had a harder life than most girls her age. Her father had left them. In a rage on a very difficult day, Adria had burned his possessions and few remaining pictures of the man who helped bring Mutton into the world.

Several times a month for the last two years, her mother would drive Mutton into Oak Corners to attend several hour-long sessions of *group therapy*, provided by the county for overweight, unhealthy teens just like herself. Mutton didn't mind these trips or even the groups. It was in these groups she heard the pain and embarrassment of overweight kids her own age. And surprisingly, she felt better. She wasn't alone. Still her mom seemed not to make the connection.

At home, Mutton was the depository for all her mother's happiness and fear. It was hard to juggle her own small life when she was regularly quizzed about what Adria had just said to her, forcing her to repeat even the simplest sentences. Sheesh! It was always about her mom and Mutton learned to tune her out. How could anyone keep up with her Mom's non-stop talk about things that had happened to her when she was young and her plan to get them out of this town to a better place. Each day she saw her frightened little mother slip back into her fear and *inertia*. "It's easy to talk about goals but if you never started them, what was the point?"

Mutton loved her mother deeply. Beautiful Adria was her safe spot. Nothing mattered when she put herself into her mom's arms. They fit together and Mutton would *chide* herself if she became impatient with her struggling mother. She had to hold it together for her mother's sake. Unfortunately, this meant playing along with Adria's whims. Mutton knew this overeating was no good for her yet somehow it made her mother calm down a bit. A small price to pay, right? "But what about me?" she asked herself.

When Mutton was a toddler, Adria would make shadow animals on the wall at night if neither could fall sleep. Adria played the wolf who saved her little sheep; a part Mutton played *literally* and *figuratively*. Mutton would bunch her little hands in the shadow game to look like balls of wool and forgetting the sounds a sheep makes, would meow or bark. They would laugh hysterically together, and

45

these were the memories Mutton would recall when she was angry or troubled even now as she grew older.

These days, her mother insisted her Mutton was always in a dark mood on the ride home from therapy. Mutton disagreed each time as was their habit, but she was *vetoed* by her very-thin parent. Adria would take Mutton to the Dairy Queen for a big cheeseburger, a chocolate shake, and a large-size fries, "to quiet her anger and sadness," Adria said. Mutton had tried to explain to her *assertive* mother how eating after food therapy wasn't healthy for her. Adria angered, spitting the tobacco bits from her constant cigarette, responded, "I'll never bring you a treat again, then. If I didn't do this for you," she warned, "you'd go home feeling sorry for yourself and I won't have it. Trust me I'm your mother, I'm an adult, and I know you."

The additional heavy weight of guilt caused by trying to please her mother despite its effects, *seesawed* through her mind and body. She always caved to her mother's anger. She loved her mother even more than herself, knowing no one else in the world had her concerns at heart. It was just so difficult trying to be herself and fit in with her mother's idea of a beautiful daughter. Mutton would wonder if she should have ever been born as the dried-out croplands passed the car window on their way home.

On these trips home after the weight loss sessions, Adria looked over at her daughter with satisfaction, bitterness, and a little sadness. All her life Adria had been the "pretty one." Thin in her tight blue jeans, wild thick blonde hair, and a sassy way. Wherever she went in those young days, men paid attention to her, asking her to dance. They wanted to take her away on a trip someplace exciting, they said. Though these trips never happened, Adria had loved the constant attention. She could not admit how much she missed her youth, but it was constant in her mind. In every cheap pair of jeans and sandals, in the pitiful condition of her single-wide trailer, Adria was reminded there was no longer any potential in her life. This was it. Enough to live on but not enough to really live.

Sadly, she regarded Mutton with satisfaction because her daughter would never be any competition. She regarded Mutton with bitterness because she, Adria, would never be young again and never again have the same potential Mutton had right now. Adria's sadness however was reserved for herself. When she had an opportunity to introduce Mutton to people, one of the first things she shared was her constant concern about her little girl's health. She would never let Mutton be the person the girl needed to be, to maintain the attention the grown woman needed to receive as the mother of a sick child.

Long ago, a newly graduated, young male therapist had brought all of this to Adria's attention. He explained kindly, how Adria was using Mutton to remain in the spotlight though at the same time keeping Mutton in an unhealthy state. Adria, shocked by his cleverness and her exposure, never saw this therapist again. Afterward, Mutton only attended these *non-judgmental* support groups, filled with other kids who were obese and desperate to please their parents by changing their appearance. Many of the kids were in pain and they wept frequently during and after the groups. Mutton was no different and she knew she belonged with the group. There she could turn herself inside out, sharing her dreams, and the difficulty of dealing with her mother.

Like many children, Mutton had long ago made a deal with herself to thwart her mother's methods. She would not eat the treats herself, bought with the money her mother gave her. She would give all the candy away to her friends. If she failed and ate even one bite of the sweets, she devised a method to punish herself. Mutton was strong though and she rarely punished herself.

Nowadays there was another huge problem for Mutton to consider. Can you believe it? Something new and truly wonderful for a best friend was becoming a cruel reality affecting Mutton's picture of herself.

Her good friend Cascade had blossomed into a beautiful young woman, even though Mutton knew Cascade had been a boy, which made it even worse. This hurt so much more than she could tell anyone including her mother or share in her obesity group. It was easy to dream you were beautiful until you stood next to a beautiful girl. The awareness that her best friend was the one to unconsciously betray her made her days even more difficult. How do you celebrate the success of someone who makes you look worse? It became obvious, by other's indirect comments, Mutton would never be pretty or hold hands with a boy after school. Mutton felt something turn within her and it also began to unravel her view of herself as a good person.

Though she was happy and proud of her friends, Ozzie and Arlo, and all still grieving for Gunther, Mutton's change meant she had to confront what was real. Worse, what everyone around her saw. She was no longer special just because she could buy her friends with a snack. Arlo wanted to treat now with his new pocket money, and funny guy, he insisted his friends eat fruit. No one seemed to mind or look to Mutton for sugary snacks anymore. No one looked at her at all anymore. Even Mr. Johnson had switched his attention, so it seemed, as everyone regarded Arlo as a generous friend and Ozzie as a hero.

On the most recent ride home from her weight group, Mutton smiled to herself happily. She'd been there when they found the money. They'd all gone into the house together and at first searched cautiously among the furniture, pulling out nearly empty drawers, and pushing aside the dishes, pots, and pans. The kids all grew impatient believing absolutely there must be a fortune hidden somewhere in Gunther's house. This belonged to Arlo and would change his life. Maybe their lives would change.

The modest old house was minimally furnished. After the search through the furniture, pulling out drawers, checking upper shelves and even pulling things away from the wall to check the wallboard, the group of kids encouraged by Mr. Johnson, still weren't ready to give up.

Ozzie ordered them all sit down in the little living room and try to relax. He wanted them to close their eyes and take several deep breaths. Each one, even Mr. Johnson, did as Ozzie directed. Then the boy asked them some questions in his calming preacher's voice.

"We know Gunther was a smart man, but he had spells. First," Ozzie said, "he would have to remember the place he put the money. Second, the money would have to be in a waterproof place. Right? Third, it would have to be in a place which could not burn, and finally it would have to be in a place Arlo would find if Gunther was unable to tell him. Right? "Also," he said thoughtfully chewing his

49

thumb again, "it might need to be in a very quick place. If Gunther needed to leave or he was sick, he would need to put his hands on the money quickly. Right?"

The young boy was never more certain and focused. He was excited about their search knowing all this made sense. Unless of course there was no money stashed away for Arlo's future. Ozzie knew his mission was to motivate the searchers and just like that, Ozzie knew he'd make his life's work motivating the tired and worn out to become something more than they expected of themselves. This felt good!

"Let's start the search again. Remember, no fire, no water, sort of out in front of us somewhere in this house, and a place you can grab quickly. Right?"

It took another hour as the children moved inside and outside the house, around the barn, garden, and shed, perplexed by this hidden treasure but eager to help Arlo. It was getting dark, and the house was close and airless against the summer heat and quite stifling. The children themselves were covered with dust, and a little bit saddened. Maybe Gunther had spent all the money. Maybe Arlo's mom's friend was lying. Worse, what if Arlo's mom had lied about sending the money?

Then Arlo screamed. It wasn't a happy scream and so it filled them all with dread. What had he found? They ran in the direction of his scream, onto the enclosed back porch. They found Arlo pulling desperately at a metal tin from a vintage icebox. The kind of icebox having a place on top for ice and a bin at the bottom for more ice or meat. The tin bin had been welded shut but it was easily pulled from the inside of the old refrigerator, and they could see one part had already been pried open.

Waterproof right? Fireproof right? Easily removed when someone needs to escape. And something unused in a house with very little furniture and a small working fridge in the kitchen. Ozzie was triumphant! He was successful and triumphant in his faith.

"My grandpa meant me to find this." Arlo sunk to his knees with his thin arms wrapped around the small metal box. And then Arlo did the strangest thing. He began to scream, horrible screams not in happiness, and not in sadness, but with a desperation none of his friends had seen before. He wailed though looking at no one, his tears and snot dropping onto the tin bin, as he choked out more words.

"Why? Why? Why do we live like this? Why did my grandpa have to live like this? Why did my mother have to leave me? Why are we all stuck here? If there's nothing in this container it's proof we're lost. No one is looking for us, and no one's ever coming to help us. We help each other but no one outside this town helps us." He held the box as one holds a baby to their chest, his body was wracked by now, silent sobs, and his tears continued to flow freely. We sat down around him, holding our breath and once again, not knowing what to do.

"I've looked after Gunther since I can remember. I've looked after him when he was wild and crazy, and I thought he'd take my head off. He didn't know what he was doing, I know this, and I knew it as a young kid. I hugged his old gray head, when he was crazy like this, and I put a cold wet rag on him. He'd soon get calm. BUT I'M JUST A LITTLE KID!! I'M SO TIRED. I'm just a kid. We're all just kids. Why is it like this?" Arlo continued to sob, his face a puffy red mess. His thin arms clenching the box, as he kept his eyes shut

We watched sadly. We didn't know what to do. Mr. Johnson put his large hand on Arlo's frail shoulder. No one moved, no one spoke. For a moment we all forgot the bin as he knelt in a sparkling clean porch in the middle of nowhere, in a town where strangers never stopped. Each one of us had our own hopes and dreams. We too were often preoccupied as Arlo was now. Being forgotten had worried us all. We relied on each other, and our youthful, naive optimism was some reassurance the dark dreams weren't real and someday something would change for good.

Chapter 7: Riley and Arlo become brothers. Abby opens a flower stand, then closes it.

The child welfare people had come and gone. Their new short-term decision was to place Arlo in Abby's care. Abby had pleaded with the local agency contact to bring Arlo into her home as she hoped it would help stabilize Riley and not dislocate the other boy prematurely from the community he loved and where he was loved. She talked to others who supported her request and Arlo became part of her simply wonderful, slightly odd, but loving household.

Arlo and Riley were good for each other. They were both intelligent young kids who had grown up without siblings and were quite independent but aware they did not have all the answers.

Soon Abby started dreaming of a small business she and Riley could run to generate more money for his education and care. Feeling her life's joy, beyond Riley, was gardening, she decided to increase her efforts and grow fruit and flowers for the town. Even the truckers at the diner might be wanting a fresh apple or pear with their usual road-diner food.

Three weeks earlier she had enlisted Ozzie to help her design and build two small movable stands. Ozzie thoughtful as always considered the needs of his client, for yes, Abby offered him a few dollars for his efforts. His first payday and he was delighted too, as Joseph had been a carpenter.

The final creations were vintage bookshelves on wheels with long battered stairwell posts as handles to maneuver them about. In all the sorrow over Gunther's death Abby had placed the stands back in her dilapidated garage until a better time. Now, with two young boys in her care, she was certain the fruit and veg stands would be a success. It was almost so at first and then wasn't after all, but for now, let's check back in with Arlo.

Arlo had loved staying with Juno, Olive, and Cascade. Unfortunately, the young, high strung, gentle boy knew he had not been a good guest with his night terrors, his crying, and the destruction of some objects he knew he had to replace when he could.

True to their nature, Juno and Olive were always busy with their craft and art business. They traveled weekly making short trips around the state, sometimes taking Cascade and Arlo along. The two young children liked each other but their physical closeness made the adult women uneasy about continuing to provide Arlo with a home. When Abby approached them one day in the small store, they were pleased with her request to care for Arlo and promised to make his transition easy; offering to provide additional meals, laundry service, and occasionally the parental attention both children required and desired.

Everyone it seems appreciated Arlo's move to Abby and Riley's except perhaps Cascade. She missed having someone her age near her and her feelings for Arlo had intensified. Among her old troubles, she was experiencing her first loss and possibly her first love. Cascade looked forward to their easy-going conversations and even when neither had anything to say, they enjoyed each other's quiet company. Cascade never had to explain herself to Arlo.

"Growing up is complicated," Cascade moaned often. Her moms made life easier it was true and never hovered or invaded her privacy. She could be herself now, dressing as she wished. Also, the women's intense relationship didn't

leave as much time for her as she'd liked up until the last few months. Now it gave

her a sense of freedom she didn't know she'd appreciate. Almost the whole day

could go by before the moms checked in on her. This no longer stressed Cascade

out and her new maturity pleased both her mothers.

But Arlo. Dear sweet, skinny, Arlo. He was another head full of

consideration indeed. She loved how Arlo accepted and appreciated her. Even in

their small friendly town, Cascade was aware a few people did not want her lesbian

moms out and about. Adding to this reallization, people, mostly men, would slow

their cars to get a glance at Cascade if she ventured from her moms' house and art-

filled yard. Arlo made her feel safer and maybe, just maybe, the thought of him

kept her from running away again with the suitcase she had repacked and hidden in

the small shed which was her "playhouse."

It would have been easier if there was anyone like her in town. Cascade

planned on asking Mutton if she could sit in on her youth therapy groups. Did they

cover subjects other than weight loss? It seemed to her lots of kids in her grade

school could do with some therapy time. The adults weren't generally ready to talk

except give directions. Where was the "why and how" most kids wanted to talk and

learn about? "Just listen sometimes, and not offer advice," Cascade begged her

moms from time to time.

Arlo too had considered asking Mutton and Gunther if he could attend

these groups. He had a lot of questions and the adults around him were often silent

and overly protective. They gave warnings, often without saying why, and they restrained all the kids from really busting out. It was a good thing sometimes Arlo reasoned, and he took advantage of this to say what he needed to say usually at the wrong time. He grew louder and more frustrated when they tried to shush him. He'd push back and catch them off guard.

Now, at home with Abby and Riley, Arlo could ask many questions, and Abby and Riley would try to answer and reason along with him. With his grandfather, Arlo had been afraid of Gunther's temper, his dark moods, and the nights the old man literally howled at the moon. Here at Abby's, all was peaceful. Riley and Abby snored loudly at night, but he grew accustomed to it, even relieved to know these loving people were close by.

Arlo's *miniscule* room was across from Riley's and Abby moved onto an old sofa jammed into a crook in the hall between them. As Abby slept soundly the two boys would sneak back and forth into each other's rooms, talking quietly until it was very late. Neither had realized immediately that their friendship could become even more important and without the pressure of assisting Gunther, Arlo began to calm down.

Riley loved having an older brother now and he too, got a great deal of support from Arlo with Abby. His small, rounded shoulders began to loosen, and he reacted less dramatically to events around him. When Abby woke in the middle of the night to water her garden in the cool breeze, she'd find both boys wrapped in blankets sleeping head-to-toe, as Arlo's moods improved quickly at his new home.

Missing Cascade however made his heart ache. It made him feel unwound and he struggled for breath when he thought about her. Cascade challenged to him to think harder and be more mature. He failed often but it didn't drive Cascade away as it did with the other kids in his classroom. She "got" him. Was this love? It was mighty powerful and if Cascade left him, as she had tried a few times by thumbing a ride on the interstate, he knew he'd have to go find her.

Arlo didn't understand why people in town rejected Cascade and her moms. He'd give anything to know someone cared enough when he took a bath and brushed his teeth. The fridge food was there, and his sheets were clean, made his life so much easier and his anxiety dropped a quite a bit.

One morning, Abby announced she had a plan. She was going to put them all to work. They'd love it, she said with careful pride and simple delight. It was time.

The first day, under Abby's direction they loaded up the two carts with fresh fruit and vegetables. Purple plums and bright yellow pears from her trees, massive and tiny red tomatoes from the sunny side of the garden, and big bunches of wildflowers plucked gently from her garden. She guided Riley over to Mr. Johnson's little store and set him up in front with a badly written poster advertising their products. The little boy was taking his role very seriously and as soon as Abby and Arlo left, he began to shout like a *barker* advertising the goods for sale.

Abby and Arlo headed over to the truck stop diner. There she chose a place just off the front entrance giving Arlo some small coins and singles to make change for the customers.

It wasn't long however, though before there was trouble. It was a total surprise and put the small trio into confusion and shock.

Mr. Johnson appeared at the diner, dragging Riley behind him. He beckoned to Miss Abby. Soon enough the owner of the truck stop diner came out to inspect this new arrangement. He and Mr. Johnson directed Abby over to them, away from the setup so the young boys wouldn't hear them file their very disappointing complaints.

"Miss Abby, we know you have your problems, but you don't have a *business license* and truly your business competes with ours. This is a small town and there aren't many customers coming through and now we got more competition," said the owner of the diner. "You'll just have to move along now and take this junk with you."

Arlo watched unaware he was reading the men's lips. He could see Miss Abby was beginning to wilt physically and her hand was tight on her own throat. Without a second's hesitation the boy loped over and stood up to the men. He began yelling, "this is America, and everybody deserves a chance. Everyone in a small town must stick together." Squaring his shoulders, he glared at the two taller men.

A small crowd began to move outside from within the diner. The young boy explained to the people the problems both Abby and her young charges had overcome just to get to this place. And their very own neighbors and friends were stopping them. "Does this behavior make you angry?" he demanded of the crowd.

The owner was embarrassed and began to get cross. "Abby I'm going to ask you one more time to move along or I'll have to call the sheriff's deputies. It's not pleasant but it's the law." He strode swiftly back inside his diner to place a call.

Abby was completely defeated and shakily stood, quiet tears running down her cheeks, her arm around Arlo. Mr. Johnson pushed Riley to the center with the second cart.

"Miss Abby, you, and I have been looking after each other for many years now. We both have struggles and somehow, we overcome the best we can. You have young people to take care of and I've got to manage my store. It's all I've got now." Mr. Johnson shrugged his *ancient* shoulders looking as defeated as Abby. His large hand was on Riley's shoulder and the boy began to cry, overcome with helplessness. Both he and the old man were on the verge of one of their emotional fits.

A marked car drove up. The young sheriff's deputies were both acquainted with Abby and Riley from the little boy's episodes. The owner of the diner came out trying to explain his position and apologizing to the whole crowd and showing more *deference* to Abby. Abby didn't speak the whole time. She was dazed and her lips moved silently in some pitiful speech which failed to motivate her to be assertive. Abby was sweating *profusely* and taking short, sharp breaths.

The confrontation began to draw a larger crowd. This was exciting stuff for their little town. People from further down the Main Street walked up to find out what was going on and the crowd grew noisy. Reflected in their faces was the sadness and loss of hope in a friend's frustration. Many had tried, as Abby was doing, to create something new, to generate a few bucks, and add a little dignity back to their life. They were all tired and many wiped tears from their own eyes as they realized even good ideas weren't allowed to them and life would go on as it always had with neglect and fear.

Cascade too had been drawn to the crowd by the raised voices and she immediately understood the feelings Arlo had expressed sometime earlier. No one cared for them, and they'd never get out of here.

She raised her arms above her head, giving a shout and drawing the crowd's attention to her. "When is it our turn" she asked? "When do we get a shot at life? If we can't do this little thing together, we don't stand a chance."

She gestured to the diner owner and to Mr. Johnson, asking, "where do you buy your vegetables and fruit? Where do you buy the flowers, you put on your tables and Mr. Johnson why aren't you selling flowers? It seems to me it's in your best interest to make Miss Abby your supplier! She's a local and she's your friend and more importantly she's a person in great need! You both can help not just one or two, but many people in this town. You hire people from Oak Corners, you buy vegetables from some far away company when we have small farmers here, and excellent produce right here in town! WHY AREN'T YOU HELPING US?!?" she roared.

The crowd erupted into applause and shouts. The deputies nodded their heads in agreement. This was a handy solution, and surprisingly it came from a kid.

The irate red-faced owner of the diner replied angrily, "you don't understand what business is all about. Tell them, Mr. Johnson, about the long-term relationships and *credit* we have with our *suppliers*."

Mr. Johnson just hung his head, gesturing toward the diner owner as a sign of agreement. The crowd now of almost 50 people, booed. The deputies didn't like this turn of events. They began to raise their own arms to move the loud group of people away from the diner's entrance, but this only seemed to make people more defiant.

The folks began to shout, and a few sat down on the ground in protest of the deputies' authority. They expected an answer, a good answer. The deputies were unprepared with a soothing answer. And then, it got worse.

"Hear me, gentlemen. We won't buy from you, we won't spend money with you, and we're going to tell everybody this isn't a good place to eat. If you can't support the community the community will not support you. Miss Abby isn't looking to make a fortune. She's trying to raise two young boys in a place where no one is doing so well. Isn't it time we stuck together?" Olive in denim *coveralls* stood strong in front of the deputies with her arms crossed against her chest, her brilliant red lips pursed, and her dark eyes deadly and determined. She'd done this before in her early life when she was alone or in a company attempting to make some changes for the better. Olive could out talk most people in her sleep when equal rights were at question.

The crowd, no longer moving at the deputies' request, cheered.

Olive entreated Mr. Johnson, "Tell us how it works Mr. Johnson." she held up her thumb. "this is me Mr. Johnson. Your thumb is you; my thumb is me."

Next, she held up her thumb and index finger. "This, Mr. Johnson is you and the diner."

She extended her middle finger alongside her extended thumb and index finger, "this is my emotion Mr. Johnson, because of you. You have engaged me today with your behavior and it affects me, and it makes me angry and sad how you can stand there and tell us you want to pay some nameless big company when you have a perfectly good supplier as a friend."

"What am I going to do about this Mr. Johnson? I'm going to raise my ring finger, and this is a reaction to my emotion, like you taught me, Mr. Johnson. My reaction, Mr. Johnson, is to tell you I will now do my shopping far, far away and you the owner of our diner, the largest business in our little town, you will no longer see me inside when I have a few bucks in my pocket to take my family out to dinner. I'm done spending money in this town if we can't all support each other."

"If we can't step in and help each other then this town is truly destroyed and those are the consequences today, gentlemen, of your actions towards this woman and her attempts to raise two children. You know what happens in small towns? We talk, and we talk a lot, and we will talk to everyone we can between here and the state border and they will know there is nothing in this town worth stopping for!"

The crowd was silent now. This was a different very *provocative* approach, and it was unexpected. So many of the townspeople had lived without hope and a complete sense of despair but full-on rebellion was unexpected. They weren't too sure about this change in the wind's direction and for those without transportation, Mr. Johnson's was the only store in town. The crowd searched each other's faces for an answer. Wasn't there a better way?

As the crowd began to mumble, Juno came and stood close to her partner, her arm around their daughter Cascade. The three women looked tough, and the crowd swung their heads in their direction.

"Look people we have a business, and we must go outside of town to get customers to sell our goods. BUT WE SPEND OUR MONEY HERE! Most of you don't respect us, most of you don't look at us, and many of you have been rude to our daughter. We CAN leave, and some of you cannot. If you don't begin to support the community, it will become even less than it is now. I suggest each and every one of you who has a craft, good health, and a few bucks, start packing up. This isn't going to get any better, my friends," Juno summarized sadly.

Arlo and Riley began to sob, wrapping their arms around the softly swaying Miss Abby, crying, and wiping their tears and runny noses onto her sleeves. The chastened crowd rose and began to disperse slowly. Abby and the boys began to push the still beautiful, untouched, fully loaded carts back in the direction of their home.

Juno and Olive stood quite still, their arms still around their young daughter. They met the eyes of anyone who gave them a *dirty look* and did not back down. Eventually the deputies convinced the two women and their daughter to head home.

A few people in the crowd were angry how the lesbian couple had the *gall* to preach to them. Hadn't they too been living through this? Some people don't like being shown their fear and instead of motivating them to change, they decide to "*kill the messenger.*"

Chapter 8: Cascade's house burns down. Cascade and Mutton may have the same father.

Later that month, Juno begged a ride from Adria to Oak Corners. They agreed to go the same day Mutton attended her groups and Cascade insisted she go along too. It was Cascade's *adamant* plan of action she would join Mutton simply to see if there was anything there for her needs and emotions.

Both moms agreed and they started off early on a hot humid day. Without air conditioning the only way to keep the old car bearable was to drive fast and Adria did the best she could on the interstate. Once they got close to Oak Corners, she slowed the car to avoid a speeding ticket. The engine immediately began to make *erratic* noises and the ride became bumpy. Adria got the car to the side of the road just as the engine gave up. Jumping out quickly the small gang ran under a small group of forlorn trees to protect themselves from the sun and intense heat if they could.

In the beginning, not one vehicle slowed for them. No sheriff's deputies were in sight.

The stranded girls were determined to meet their goals to attend a group today and suggested they too could stand at the side of the road to thumb a ride. Their surprised and dismayed mothers *rejected* this immediately and the adults took up a spot just before the broken-down car. Passing cars and trucks hooted their horns though no one stopped until a van slowed. The driver, a man with *aviator sunglasses*, slowed and pulled over just beyond the broken-down car. He turned the van's engine off and slowly walked back towards the women. The young girls ran out from under the trees to make sure they would get a ride.

In barely a second, Adria, running, threw her arms around the tall man, both laughing happily.

He was suntanned, wearing jeans and a worn t-shirt. Cascade noticed his hair immediately. He was beautiful in her mind. Blonde hair, lean, and friendly. And Adria knew him. Well, well. This was an interesting trip today. Life outside Neezer was picking up noticeably.

Mutton ran ahead and she threw her arms around the man. He hugged her, picking her up to swing her in a full circle as the three laughed and talked excitedly. Cascade joined them with a big smile. She'd certainly get to a group today, fingers crossed.

Only Juno stood back. She continued searching for oncoming cars pretending to ignore the trio dancing happily together. Cascade wasn't having it.

"Mom, c'mon. Say hello for chrissake! This is our only chance to get to town and maybe back." Juno glanced back at her sadly, shrugging, and shielding her eyes from the sun and her daughter.

Adria dragged the man back to meet Juno and Cascade. He came happily and then as he approached the second mother-daughter group, he slowed, grew serious, then laughed out loud.

"Juno Whitby! Wow, what are the chances? You know Adria and my daughter, Catherine (Mutton)? Dang, I had no idea you'd come back to our sorry patch from the excitement of Los Angeles. Didn't work out for you?"

66

This man, Greg reached out to hug Juno, who held herself stiffly but lightly patted his shoulders in his deep bear hug.

"Juno, who is this? Your daughter?" He paused and repeated "daughter" with more certainty. "What are you up to hanging out with Adria?"

Adria stepped between them and introduced Greg, who was Mutton's father. Adria attempted to explain. "Greg and I spent some time together and we both knew he was gay. He wanted kids too, so I obliged him. And now we have our beautiful Mutt., I mean Catherine."

She turned her attention to Greg. "How's Ray? What are you two up to these days?"

All this time, Greg had his eyes fixed on Juno then Cascade. He kept looking back and forth between the two. Then he shook his head, saying quietly, "it's a great pleasure to see you again and meet your beautiful daughter. Are you kids friends too?"

Cascade launched herself forward to explain "they had an appointment in Oak Corners, and he could see"…and she gestured to his van.

"Of course," Greg said. "Let's get you into town and we can figure the car out later." The four women piled into the van and Gregg settled into the driver's seat still chatting though his eyes were locked on Cascade most of the time.

Juno was silent and shut her eyes as if napping. Mutton watched both Greg and Cascade. They just stared at each other. She was angry, really angry. Why was her dad paying more attention to Cascade than to his own daughter. Not fair! It's never fair! Mutton closed her eyes tightly to keep from crying.

Adria kept interrupting him to explain to the others how he'd run off with a few people to LA. "But there's no place like home, right?" The three adults laughed bitterly at their own joke. And Cascade began putting it together. Her mom, Juno had gone off to LA with Gregg. She'd never been told this she just simply knew it right now. "Think," she told herself. "Something's wrong here."

"Not if I can help it," Mutton said to herself later that night as she lay in bed. All her dad did was pay attention to Cascade. He asked HER questions about school, HER friends, and the boredom everyone felt in Neezer Place. It had been his home too many years ago. He and his partner Ray had met in Los Angeles and after a time of surfing and bartending they had left for New Mexico. Now he was back near his home and seeing his daughter Catherine and her mother Adria each month if their schedules worked out.

She was not going to share this man, her father, with the very beautiful Cascade. For a moment, she allowed herself the pleasure of imaginary revenge. Then she fell asleep convinced she would do anything to keep her father to herself.

Later…Cascade was choking, waking quickly from her sleep. She jumped up when she realized the smoke was real and she thought she could hear what sounded like wood burning rapidly. She frantically stumbled down the stairs quickly and found both her mothers still asleep.

Shaking them in fright and fear, she tried to scream but her throat was dry from the smoke she had already inhaled. She continued to cry and choke as the women were slow to respond. Once awake though they leapt from the bed and grabbed Cascade, pushing her out the front door.

The entire back of their small house was engulfed in flames. Cascade ran around the outside and she could see her playhouse, the shed, and their van in flames. Seconds later, the van exploded, and fireballs roared through the air, landing on the sunburnt brush and trees around their house. The dry grass was soon in flames and the three women ran further to the road for safety.

The volunteer Fire Marshalls did their best to contain the fire. It was no use as the house and the grounds had been burning for almost 20 minutes before the pumper arrived. Fire trucks from other towns came later but only to keep the fire from going further. The house and their possession were just a few burned beams and unidentifiable smoking piles. Everyone was in shock.

Juno and Olive stood across the road with their arms around Cascade. They cried desperately over the loss of their home, possessions, and the means of their livelihood. How had this started? None of them smoked and they did all their cooking on an outside grill.

People wandered around in a daze. Some of the other townsfolk had come along in their nightwear and boots, shaking and their heads and shedding a few tears. The Fire Marshalls directed everyone away from the still smoldering property.

Adria and Mutton put the three women up for the night. None slept well and the next morning all of them left early to join the town at the charred site that had once been their home and workshop.

The Fire Marshall got right to the point. "Is it possible you left your welding equipment on or unprotected, ladies? The two women replied they hadn't been welding in almost a week. They continued to walk around the still smoking grounds and talking with the officials. The adults did not notice Mutton waving to Cascade join her across the small road.

Mutton got right to the point. Mutton prefaced it by saying, "I promise you I did not do this. I know who did it and he's here in the group. What should I do? Mutton and Cascade stared at each other, open mouthed, in real fear. The person who had done this was watching them even now?!?

Mr. Johnson who stood thirty feet away watched the two young women talking and gesturing frantically. This could be important, he guessed correctly. Mr. Johnson nonchalantly ambled over to them. He placed his large hands upon Cascade and Mutton's shoulders and told Cascade of his grief over the loss of her home and things.

"Do you know anything important you think the grownups should know about?" He continued glancing back and forth between the two girls.

Sitting on the neighbor's stone stoop under a rose covered arbor nearby, Arlo and Riley watched the intense conversation between the girls and Mr. Johnson. The women were serious, and the elderly Black man had an angry face. Angier than they had ever seen Mr. Johnson, though he was not angry with them it seemed. They too felt the conversation was important but as the boys joined the group the other three immediately fell silent. Mr. Johnson excused himself to the children. Walking away he beckoned to the fire marshal who joined him with a raised eyebrow.

Hours later most of the town knew the cause of the fire. This was big stuff. This was walking house-to-house-to-spread-the-word stuff.

Mutton cried through the long interview with law enforcement, begging for forgiveness. Adria listened in disbelief, her arms around her trembling daughter. They took down everything Mutton said in their notebooks. After a quiet conversation among the officials and Mr. Johnson, they agreed on a course of action. They made an arrest.

The next day…Miss Abby sat on the front steps of Mr. Johnson store. He had to explain several times what had taken place the night before as Mutton, Cascade, and the firefighters had shared information.

"Mutton was all fired up about something that happened in Oak Corners, and she went to Cascade's playhouse to leave her a note which was unkind and demanding. She said she couldn't in all her anger speak to Cascade directly and she didn't want to say anything in front of an adult. Mutton pinned the note to a bulletin board in the playhouse and left to return home. At the edge of the property, she stopped to see if anyone was around or had seen her. She was frightened when she realized someone was walking into the playhouse right then after she had just left it. She got closer to see who it was."

"Mr. Barlow, a nasty old white racist guy, was leaving the playhouse and it seems he had Mutton's letter in his hands. Within seconds, the playhouse burst into flames. Then Mutton ran home scared out of her wits not knowing what to do. I told the sheriff's deputies Mutton's story, and they immediately went to Mr. Barlow's house."

71

"And this is where things get stupid. Mr. Barlow claimed it was Mutton who started the fire and he had the note to prove she had been there. What a terrible man! Not a clue in his mean-old head! The perfectly NOT burnt letter proves HE was there AFTER Mutton, and he had no reason or rhyme to be there. Mutton was just delivering her letter and she wouldn't want it burned, would she? When the sheriff's deputies pointed this out, Mr. Barlow began cussing, saying some horrible things about Juno, Olive, and especially Cascade. He blames the decline of life in the town on lifestyles such as theirs. And get this, Barlow still had the gas cans in the back seat of his car. He finally confessed. Anger almost always leads to horrible consequences."

Miss Abby gave her little smile to Mr. Johnson and asked him to explain again. "Please." She continued slurping on her second bottle of orange soda. Mr. Johnson sighed and patiently started over as was his way.

Over at Adria and Mutton's trailer the five women sat cross legged in circle on a small, frayed green carpet handknitted by one of the older women in town long ago. Mutton, wrapped in her fuzzy cartoon character blanket, and Cascade with her back as straight as an arrow, stared at each other still not believing the fire had taken place. Everything, everything was gone.

Cascade's moms were struck dumb by the loss of their home and livelihood. There was no insurance. How would they start over?

Adria was wondering if she should drop the final bomb. She kept her eyes on Juno the whole time then decided to break the silence.

"Listen ladies, I have some important news. It's sort of good and it's not bad but compared to the last 24 hours I think it's important to agree we all stand together and help each other whatever happens from this day on."

The others looked at her wearily. Adria gestured with her chin towards Juno and inquired if it would be OK to share her information. Juno put up a hand helplessly, pulling Cascade into her arms, kissing her multiple times on the top of her still-smokey blonde head.

"I guess it's alright. But maybe I should tell the story. I don't know for sure because I truly thought those days were in the past, "said Juno.

Over the next hour Juno explained her childhood in this town and the friends she had then and now. Olive and Cascade began to learn many new things about Juno, her family, and this town as it used to be.

Juno had met Greg during high school in Oak Corners. She had always been attracted to him and even when he came out as gay with Ray much later, she decided her life was better knowing him than without him. Juno had left with a small group, including Greg, in an old station wagon the night of high school graduation to try their luck in Los Angeles.

On their small savings, the group made it to LA before the car self-destructed and they were left to live on the beach. It had been a perfectly wonderful time with lots of beautiful young people with no care in the world, waiting on tables and cleaning motel rooms to earn a living. Juno had planned to go to college after she had saved a bit of money, but things don't always work out.

One warm August morning on the beach, Juno woke up in Greg's arms, feeling odd, and knowing immediately she was pregnant. She told no one. Pretending to go to work, Juno stuffed all her money in her pocket, and went to the Greyhound Bus pickup point four blocks away. Five hungry days later she was back in Neezer Place. She stayed with an older woman, Ondine, who had knitted her a blanket much like the carpet on the floor, in town until her baby was born. Juno stroked Cascade's hair and pulled her child even closer.

Adria interjected. "I got pregnant with Greg's child a few months before high school graduation. That's why he left. He was scared and uncertain about liking boys or girls. He sent me money after Mutt…, I mean Catherine was born. Ray has welcomed both of us."

Juno responded, "I didn't know what to do. I worked at the truck stop as many hours as I could and decided to leave for Oak Corners but wound up in the state capital. Don't ask. There, I ran into Olive demonstrating against government oppression and women's rights. We hit it off. She and the baby loved each other."

"When Olive asked me to follow her, I did, and we've traveled all over even to the East Coast. It was exciting, but it was rough having a child on the road with no regular home, no clean bathroom, or bank account. Olive came here with me because I asked her too. She's given up so much for Cascade and me. I know I wouldn't have survived if she hadn't been there for us. Even yesterday she made a bigger sacrifice than I or anyone can imagine."

Juno and Olive stared at each, wiping tears away. Their commitment touched everyone they met.

74

"What can I say? Neezer is an inexpensive place to live, and I imagined we'd only be here for a full year. Save some money and get Cascade walking.

Juno lapsed back into silence. Everyone was staring at the small, frayed carpet beneath them.

Adria spoke first. "There's more you and I know, and you need to tell us. Greg and I think we know the answer but only you know if it's true."

Juno sighed deeply. "What you should know, and I did not know until yesterday when we met Greg on the road is Cascade and Catherine are half-sisters. You both have Greg as a father."

The surprised women remained seated not saying a word, resisting the heat and humidity of the trailer. They were at a loss for words and too tired to think clearly.

The next day, Olive, Juno, and Cascade moved into Gunther and Arlo's old house. Arlo said, "he wouldn't charge any rent if Cascade stayed in town. At least for a while," he said, blushing and looking away *nonchalantly*.

Chapter 9 Mr. Johnson, the two men, and the death of a friend

Trouble likes to find quiet places to make itself known. The world intrudes everywhere, and we must find a way to create a safe place in our community and in our hearts. It wasn't the end of trouble for Neezer Place. The spirits of Neezer see everything and tell no one.

The two young bikers laughed at Mr. Johnson as he stumbled around behind his battered store counter, appearing helpless when adding up their purchases and making change. They gave sly looks at each other, nudging and smirking to show their superiority over this *decrepit* old man. The tall one coughed and gestured to the short one as he dropped a couple of beef jerky sticks into his shirt pocket without offering to pay for them.

The stillness became *unbearable*. And this was the moment everything changed. "Enough," said Mr. Johnson jerking his head in the man's direction and becoming utterly still. The two strangers froze still smirking. It wasn't a good day for Mr. Johnson, yet he was still sharp in all the necessary ways.

"What are you going to do about it, old man?" the short one sneered. Mr. Johnson blinked and shrugged, then continued to bag the men's groceries. He proceeded slowly, taking his time with each item, placing it carefully into wrinkled brown paper bags. Time dragged and the two bikers rolled their eyes at each other, not bothering to hide their disgust.

Quietly without drawing attention or warning, Mr. Johnson raised a large ancient black pistol from behind the two brown bags. His hands were no longer shaking, and he said low and carefully, "you owe me another fifty cents, Sir."

The men looked at each other. Surprise, surprise. Well, they knew what to do.

Just minutes later, Riley stepped into the quiet store. "Mr. Johnson, I'm here. Miss Abby needs two cans of tuna fish, sir." No response. Unusual as Mr. Johnson always locked up even for a short lie-down break in the back room. Odd. Riley peered down the empty, quiet aisles, all three of them. No one.

Grabbing the two cans off the shelf Riley began to write a note at the counter to Mr. Johnson when he heard a low moan come from behind the counter. Checking quickly, Riley found the old Black man, seated on the floor, legs splayed, eyes closed, as Mr. Johnson clutched his chest. Riley grabbed the phone and called the sheriff's deputies.

Later…"Please go children. Please go," the young Black woman cooed to the crying children. I'll let you know what's up later. I'll find out what's happening." The young woman who shooed them out the front door, was Mr. Johnson's niece, Tracey. She'd driven over from Oak Corners as soon as the deputies showed up at her door.

The EMT workers had tried to keep Mr. Johnson alive on the way back to Oak Corners but he kept failing. Some intensive *CPR* and two or three times using the *defibrillator* didn't do any good. As they pulled into hospital emergency entrance the old man wheezed and life as we know it, left him.

Sometimes all a community knows is grief. Even the happy events, the birth of a child, or the meeting of two old lovers has a bittersweet tang but the town as witness must attend to the events as necessary to show respect and perhaps participate in the sad excitement. We all know pain and in sharing, we find our pain a bit more bearable.

They held Mr. Johnson's funeral days later in Oak Corners. Almost all Neezer Place carpooled or hitchhiked to the solemn affair at the New Angel Baptist Church. It seems many Neezer residents owed the generous Mr. Johnson money and townspeople gave beat-up bags of coins to his family in repayment from guilt and grief.

The gang of kids bawled silently during the celebration of Mr. Johnson's life and the music was solemn, sad, and joyful all at the same time. Boxes of tissues were passed around the old church and by this gesture the people connected.

The church ladies had been warned and they met the challenge. The large church garden, shaded by old oaks and fir trees, was filled with tables covered in food and soft drinks, sweet rolls, and cookies. Several large hams and many sausages made mouths water for most had never seen such a feast.

Wise folk had brought garden and folding chairs, and they offered these to the elderly. Some *experienced* people brought blankets and those without just sat on the flattened summer-dried grass in small groups. Conversations varied and though some spoke sadly about the man, others laughed and told loving jokes about him. Women, old and young, passed plates of cakes and cookies around and the food never seemed to diminish.

Cascade and Catherine, now almost joined at the hip, sat with their little group in a circle of thanksgiving. "What were we grateful for on this day?" asked Catherine.

Arlo, not his usual reactive self, paused to think deeply instead of blurting out everything on his mind this day. "I think I am grateful for the adults in our lives who despite their own problems managed to keep us all safe." His thoughts were about Mr. Johnson, and especially about the care his sick Grandfather Gunther and his desperate mother had taken despite being overcome themselves. He reflected on his new financial condition after finding the money his mother had so thoughtfully squirreled away. Perhaps she did it to make amends and resolve her guilt for leaving him, her little boy, behind.

Riley said he was grateful for all of them. "I'm the smallest in the group and you still let me hang out with you. None of the other big kids would let me in. You're my family and will always be. We have to keep looking after each other." They all nodded their heads in agreement.

Ozzie had carried his Bible all day long. He spoke softly, "because of you and Mr. Johnson, I know what real love and spiritual belief is about. It's not a church; it's the people in the church. No one is perfect, but because we are so messed up, we have an opportunity to be good folk and help each other. Sometimes even when we can't help ourselves. You all are the best people I know and if I have anything to do with it, none of us is going to hell. "But" he admitted, "we've got lots of living to do before our own judgment day."

Cascade and Catherine looked at each other briefly before speaking. Catherine started by saying, "I've never been happy with myself unless I think about the friends I have. Even when you stopped eating my snacks you kept looking after me, talking to me, and never making jokes about my fat. You guys are the best." Quietly hunched, she began to cry again.

Cascade took a second to look at each of her friends making direct eye contact. "If I talk too much I'm going to start crying and will not be able to stop. What's happened to all of us has not been the best of times. Please promise me you'll never let me go too far away or be alone." The last statement was directed at Arlo, and they gave each other a brief nod of agreement and promise.

The children reached out to hold hands in the circle and for the first time in their lives, it seemed they were becoming more adult. Good times bring fun and laughs but bad times bring strong attachments.

Adria, Juno, and Olive sat by themselves under the shade of a tree which insisted on shedding on them. They chatted back and forth, absentmindedly brushing the leaves and twigs off themselves. They piled the paper plates with leaves as they chatted.

"It's time to go," said Adria, thankful her old car was still functioning.

"We think you're right," said Juno. "I mean to say to you Adria, Olive, Cascade, and I will be leaving Neezer Place as soon as we can." Adria began to choke back slow tortured sobs at this news. "Sooner the better," claimed Olive, each adding their own tears of fatigue, anxiety, and hopelessness.

"Greg has offered us a place in one of their outbuildings that has a toilet and shower. We can make something of the small space because we have nothing to drag with us. Oak Corners is not the center of the world, but it has a bit more going on than Neezer ever will again. We must think about our future and find a place with more potential. We're going to look for jobs in Oak Corners and think about doing our art again. Maybe after a year we'll move on to a place with more people. Kinder people."

Olive responded, "I have to have more hope for the future and despite the few wonderful people in Neezer, I have to believe there's more happiness elsewhere."

They picked up their paper plates, laughing at how these were filled with leaves exclaiming quietly "How did that happen?" and put them in the garbage barrels near the emptying parking lot. It was time to go in so many ways. Their minds had been in so many different places and on subjects this afternoon.

Only Miss Abby seemed untouched by the death of their friend Mr. Johnson. During the service she had sung loudly, out of tune, barely remembering the words of the hymns. She had drawn smiles from the other people in the congregation, who on such a sad day realized everyone is joyful and grief stricken in different ways. During the picnic, Miss Abby had strolled the church grounds, pulling weeds, and pushing debris away with the side of her best polished combat boots. She had worn a hat because the service was in a church and her baseball cap was covered in blooms from her own garden. Still, she wasn't the oddest person there and everyone embraced her.

Chapter 10 All the kids gather at the abandoned house

"You know I can see you, don't you?" Riley stared straight at me possibly for the first time ever with his question. I giggled silently and looked across at my equally silent twin brother. He too was amused how after all these years the children had finally decided to acknowledge us.

"Is she a girl or a boy?" Cascade pointed with her chin in my direction. The group responded with either "boy or girl." Right on the mark depending which twin you were focused on.

"They could all see one of us but not all of them could see the same twin. They began to ask questions and I believe they understood we couldn't answer them. We couldn't talk or respond for living human beings to understand. We know some people could see us now and then when we pass across sunlight or a brilliant full moon. We are just some of the spirits of Neezer Place."

"Having died so many years ago, my brother and I know people sometimes see us and perhaps even shake their heads as if they're not completely sure. We're like those people you pass on the sidewalk in a busy city, you see them, but you don't really SEE them. They pass by and if they look back, and they almost never look back, we're not there anymore. The dead have different ways of appearing to the living and I don't think my brother and I were ever given a choice. We've had almost a hundred years to figure out our powers and limitations and this was it for us."

"We can't leave this town and when these children move away, we may not have anyone to follow. The town is shrinking, and no one wants to stay here with no life or future. But for some reason we must stay. We will miss them more than we've ever missed anyone in all the years we've been following people around Neezer."

Ozzie looked in my brother's direction. He said, "I know you're my guardian angel. I know you've protected me, and you even put things in my head." (We hadn't put things in his head, but I couldn't tell him so.) Ozzie continued, "I've never felt alone because of you, and it doesn't matter who you are because I know you'll always be here. I think you've been protecting all of us. Don't you guys think so too?"

Riley looked solemnly at me and said, "You're the one who makes sure I never get lost. I can only go looking for my parents because I know you're going to make sure I'm safe. I've seen you enough to know you're our age, I think."

I giggled in my soft baby voice. "Riley I can't leave this town though I have walked you to the edge of town and fortunately was there when you walked back. If you remain here, my brother and I will look after you, but if you leave you will have only the memory of us." I would miss him so much.

Riley continued, "you must look after Abby. I'm afraid I will leave here soon, and she won't be comfortable anywhere else. Can you do this, please?" the little boy implored.

My brother answered in his voice booming like thunder, "we will look after everyone in this town. You can't hear me, but I will touch your heart and you will know."

Cascade and Catherine continued to stare at me with kind interest. I smiled back and waved at them, hoping they could catch a glimpse of the movement. I would miss them both and was delighted they had found their true bond. The Dreamer and the Protector would do well together in life.

Despite the new understanding that the children could see us, a heavy veil of grief kept us from our usual joking and laughter. Mr. Johnson, Gunther, and the fire made us much more aware of the dangers around us. I though had found a new life in being embraced in this, the first part of their journey.

On this sad but loving day together, we sat on the broken concrete patio of the house that would never be lived in, listening for the drone of small planes overhead in the hot summer sky, the grasshoppers chirping wildly, and masses of bees buzzing in the tall grass of the wild overgrown lot around us.

Ozzie fiddled with his tool belt *absentmindedly*, and for the first time in our presence, took it off carefully and laid it next to him. He lay back on the hot concrete, his arms behind his head and sighed deeply, satisfied with this day. He would dwell on the past for a long time, hoping to make sense of it. Ozzie realized now how helping people was a pretty good way to spend your life. It had brought him closer to people he loved and more understanding for those who were flawed in their thoughts and actions. They were lost and he could help them. And love them.

Mutton, now Catherine, allowed Riley to hold her calm hand with his sweaty, sticky one, happy he had found some peace and how she was the source of his comfort. She blinked her tears away. Stupid tears. Why was she blubbering now? Mom would give her grief for her typical response and say she'd suffer for a good heart all her life. Always picking up broken strays.

Arlo was silent, saddened by the death of their friend, Mr. Johnson, though content the old man's niece was a younger, more peaceful, and still kind replacement for them at the store. He missed Gunther so much and on certain days felt troubled because he could have helped his grandfather more, loved him more, and shown him his love every day.

Cascade had not told the others she was leaving town soon. It wasn't a moment for another grief and besides, she wouldn't be so far away. Never too far away.

Outside the town the traffic on the one busy road past Neezer Place, was muffled by the humidity. We dozed on and off together.

The End, for now.

Renny and Jupiter

No One Knows We're Here

Stockton, California and Las Vegas, Nevada - 1993

Renny and Jupiter, two boys, are longtime friends and 6th grade classmates in Stockton California. Their parents present with *socio-economic issues* and *multiple diagnoses*, and their extended families, a mix of Black, Mexican, and Vietnamese live around them. The families though supportive of each other have conflicting and dangerous interactions, but a series of tragedies and joys bring them back together.

The boys experience their *newfound sexuality* in a place where too much information is necessary for safety but can be a hard thing for young people to manage emotionally. They fall in and out of deep friendships and their self-care overcomes their fears about and for each other. As they grow, they adopt new plans they alone will help each other experience and achieve.

Renny is a tall athletic Black/Vietnamese boy, intelligent, and *sexually conflicted*. He feels the strain of being his mom's primary concern and caregiver. Jupiter (his nickname), is a heavyset Mexican boy, overfed and indulged by a female led household. He is *philosophical, erudite*, and lapses into the "easiest way" of life. Too often he takes the *path of least resistance* due to frustrations within his community and family. The boys compare and assess, share perspectives on the benefits and hardships of crime, the lack of opportunity, and the need to avoid or embrace the chosen paths of relatives and classmates.

86

Their families, school, and law enforcement organizations provide the background in their lives, and their experiences and situations are much grittier than the other two stories in this book.

(Words in italics definitions can be found in the following Glossary.)

Renny and Jupiter

Book One

Stockton, California 1993

A Trip to Las Vegas with Relatives

Papi says, "these people want to talk about Mexicans. They act all shocked and talk about our lack of skills, so we only get to clean their motels and restaurants, and oh, so bad the Mexican drug cartels! Let me tell you Mio, these people would be better off, more realistic, if they cleaned their own banos. And the problem is not Mexican drug dealers; the whole business is built on American drug BUYERS. These young white boys and girls drive their banged up *Beemers* through bad neighborhoods looking for a way to escape the American Dream. Their parents should have taken better care of their bebes."

Renny and Jupiter listened quietly, reclining on the faded green plastic lawn chairs on Papi's sunbaked rooftop. Papi could talk like this for long periods of time, and they were patient and tired from the heat of the day.

"Instead of maids and janitors, we now own the cleaning companies, we are the contractors and builders, and the restaurant owners, yes. But we must be careful because the American Dream sucks everyone in. Grazi, my little girl is so sick now." Papi pointed with his nose downstairs to a back bedroom where Grazi slept, waiting for food, and crying for help to the bathroom. She had embraced the worst parts of the dream of success.

88

"Greedy, Mio. We are all too greedy. Me, I want to sit on my roof here, work when I can, drink a beer or two when Abuela is out playing bingo, and watch the sunflowers grow and turn. Your grandmother, aye, she has a new religion. She prays to her god to make her more money at bingo. But she's good; good and smart, my beauty. We made the *down payment* on this store with the apartment upstairs from one night of Abuela's bingo winnings. Ayyyy." Papi mopped his forehead as he turned the roasting meat on the grill. He looked gratefully out at the Vegas strip, lights shimmering in the distance, a good place for his family if they were careful.

Best friends, careful friends

"Anjelah, your boy, Renny is getting so tall! Tell him to stop, take a break, and put on a little weight. Not too much though. We don't need two Jupiters!"

Anjelah and Racca glanced at each other with smirks but no laughter. Many days, it was their shared laughter which kept them from going crazy but today both were serious. The boys were on a trip with Tio Franco, to his parents' place in Las Vegas. His parents had been on all of them to move there and make more money but not everyone was free to move about the United States so easily. The boys would attract no attention here or there, and they totally acted *Angeleno*, but their mothers had become too vigilant over the years to let go so easily today.

The change machine in the small laundromat was broken. Not just broken. The reinforced steel box was hanging from the wall by its electrical cable, having been ripped out and broken open by a car with chains on its bumper late last night. The *perps*, who both women knew, but did not associate with, had backed up at high speed through the double glass doors after closing time, damaging a few washing machines in their drunken dash for the cash. They failed at trying to tow the machine away.

The mess had been cleaned up and now the owner, Habibi, and her family were putting in new metal framed doors covered in steel mesh. They said there had not been much money in the machine, but the damage was so expensive. Insurance would not pay for it as this had happened before. If Habibi filed another insurance claim, they'd cancel her insurance. Another day in the hood.

Racca, a beautiful Mexican woman, sighed deeply, thinking of their boys and their chances to escape from this dangerous, poor area as she folded her clean clothes into a large blue plastic bag. She was saving all the money she could, and it wasn't easy. The last two motels had fired their regular help and brought in companies with *liability insurance*, training, uniforms, and *sick-leave replacements*. They gave Racca a job at the desk but no raise. She worked from 9pm until 6am, six days a week. True, fortunately, when they got burned out of their last home, the motel had generously allowed her small family to use one of the rooms for a month while she looked for another rental.

The other motels were horrible places, and it was doubtful the rooms were cleaned at all. Marquesa, the other maid, and a *drag performer* in Sacramento, said it was cheaper for the motel's owners to rip out a whole room once a year and redo it cheaply than hire daily cleaners. Bad stuff happened there and Racca did not want any part of it, good pay or not.

Anjelah, a tall, slender Vietnamese woman in her 30s, was thinking pretty much the same depressing thoughts. She was bartending afternoons at a decent saloon and diner near City Hall and the Superior Court. Lots of people dropped in from around the county for their legal cases or to file for marriage and fishing licenses. They ate massive cheeseburgers, drank a few cheap beers, and tipped very little.

Anjelah's thoughts went back to her childhood in *Saigon*. Her parents owned a small restaurant and laundry. They were happy people with their lively, seven children, plenty to eat, and a large community of friends. Things though began to change long ago, out of necessity, when they sent a young, scared Anjelah to California alone on a plane.

That important day she wore her best sundress, and pretended to be going on vacation, bringing along a small suitcase of nice clothes she'd soon outgrow quickly despite working two jobs. Then her son was born. No large family for her. It wasn't possible here with the way she had to live. She *pined* sadly as she remembered her brother, Kar, who had not survived the constant clashes with rival gangs in Stockton. Afterwards, her siblings, and parents no longer wanted to come to California. Renny's father? "Let's not even talk about him," she *grimaced*.

And then, it happened.

Marquesa, known as Billy to his family, moved nervously about his small, stifling garage apartment, gathering his thoughts. The walls were hung with pictures of famous female performers, important models, *Motown* singers, and dozens of spangled dresses. Her wig collection was on foam heads stuck on nails all over the

91

walls. Marquesa portrayed *various* women on small stages in bars around this county and the next. He had tried Los Angeles, then a break in Vegas but they had too many drag performers. New York. New York City was his next big dream.

Cleaning motel rooms and performing on stage was good work if you could get it. It was going well until Billy's Momma and her new boyfriend, Albert T., decided to visit Marquesa in Vegas. Billy had not told his mother he performed as a woman. After seeing the theater and the posters of Marquesa in her act with the others, Albert T. had taken Momma out for a drink to compose Momma's shaken nerves. They never came back to him. Billy's long apologetic letters to Momma were returned unopened.

Still, Billy had a good relationship with his ex-wife and their two kids, Sonya, and Vida. Martha had met another man who was good to Martha and the girls. Billy never wanted to see New Orleans again and Martha was not sure about any of the cities Billy performed in. She sent pictures but did not tell the twin girls about their father's work.

Now, thanks to a long walk in a dark alley several nights ago, Marquesa's life was going to get much better. As if to wash away Billy's happy yet thoroughly guilty thoughts, someone tapped lightly on the door. Billy opened the door, and there stood, Alwin, a small Black nine-year-old boy dressed in a faded superhero costume. Halloween was six months past.

"Billy, some guys came by for you this morning. I told them you weren't here like you told me so you can get some sleep. They said they had some work for you. You should go to Charlie's car place. That's all." Alwin waved to Billy and trotted back to his family in the real house upfront.

Alwin and his sister were *stand-ins* for his own kids. Alwin's parents weren't crazy about Marquesa, but Billy paid the rent on time and never brought anyone around. It was unusual someone came here but everyone in this Stockton neighborhood knew each other's business. This could be good or very bad. Billy would speak to Alwin again about these men.

On Second Thought

"Don't tell your Papi but I don't think much of Las Vegas, man," Renny picked his teeth after consuming a sizeable portion of the grilled ribs. "I mean what's so special about it. The casinos and restaurants don't let us in, or they follow us around."

Jupiter laughed. "Yeah, Renny they thought we were there for jobs. How cool is that? Nah, I like it here very much, man. My mom should find a way to get us here somehow. We could both make some good coin and then we can fly away to a better place. Let's make it happen, bro!"

Renny looked sadly at his friend. "You think it will work this time, Jupe? We've tried stuff and almost got caught. Marcio told us what he'd do to us if we tried it again. Either come work for him or stay home and in school. Now, I freak when I pass a cruiser. We're just 14, man. It's way too soon for crazy work. What are we going to do here? *Bus* tables? My mom said this town is tight. The cops and the judges know what everyone is up to."

93

"Papi, says the cops come around a few times a month and he feeds them. They leave him alone then. This town must be tight and clean or the *Federales* would shut it down and give it away to their friends. It's okay if you work within the system though. Stockton got nothing, man." Jupiter checked the grill, empty after his Papi put aside food for Abuela and fed Grazi. Maybe Renny was right. This could be just another tough town for them. Deep sigh.

"You can't see stars here," said Renny to no one. "There's too much light and scientists say it's not so good for humans. Probably worse for animals. They think it's daytime." His mom said once they moved out of Stockton, she'd let him get a dog. Now, she's getting tired of his singsong constant question of when they're really going to leave.

"Hey man, lay off the meat sauce. Last night you almost farted me out of the room!" Renny was just making a joke for Jupiter but truly, Jupiter was extremely gassy for a kid.

"Ooh, Renny can't stand my farts, but he tried to kiss me!! I think you like sharing a room with me, Smoochie Boy!" Jupiter laughed and danced as he playfully minced around the still warm, sweet-smelling grill, mocking the other boy. Flailing his floppy hands in the air, Jupiter checked to make sure Renny knew he was just giving him a hard time. They stared at each from the corners of their eyes just in case this was serious. It had happened before. One or both would blow up at each other over nothing. Many times, their moms had to stop the fighting, get them to apologize, and patch things up.

Renny *scowled*, hurt how this came up so often. It was true however, despite one *humiliating* clumsy attempt, Jupiter remained his best friend, shared his lunch, and spilled the school dirt with him. Jupiter even brought him along to Vegas, twice now. Some days they wouldn't speak to each other for no certain reason. Days would go by then one of them would show up at the other's home. Still, maybe good friends are like that.

Later, Renny could barely sleep in the room the guys shared. The apartment was air conditioned but it didn't seem to help much. Renny sighed loudly and in response, Jupiter giggled and tooted again.

Knowing More Than You Realize

Alwin sat doggedly on his front stairs. He had been ordered to stay there and go no further or he would spend long hours – probably more like five minutes – in the house doing chores. Either way, it wasn't so bad.

Inside the house, his 13-year-old sister Leontine, was finishing up her chores so she could spend the rest of the afternoon with her friends down by the sprinkler in the park. The boys in the neighborhood hung out there and this fascinated his sister far more than a sprinkler for babies. Sometimes, their mother would insist Leontine take Alwin along. He had no more interest in the sprinkler than Little Leo. Little Leo was his sister's nickname. It was just a great place to watch people. And learn lots of things. His parents had no idea what went on there and Little Leo and Alwin were in no hurry to share.

Alwin and Little Leo compared their gossip and the news around their neighborhood when their parents were busy and out of the way. Alwin was far more factual in his reporting as his sister was going through a boy crazy, romantic time these days. Her stories were all told breathlessly, highly dramatic, and even Alwin had to stop her to find out if what she said was true.

"What?! Say again, Leo. You know you're making it up, aren't you?" Alwin, small hands-on hips, would cast a gloomy, scowling face upon his big sister, learned from his mother, making them both double up in laughter and giggles.

They had an usually good relationship and Little Leo was only tough on him when she was with her friends. Alwin got it. This was her posse pose. Even his sister had to have "face."

This posse consisted of eight to ten, thirteen-year-old girls who alternately hated each other, loved each other, or missed each other depending on the prevailing social crisis. Alwin thought it was a lot of useless drama and even he *pursed* his lips and rolled his eyes with his parents as Little Leo spoke and *gestured dramatically putting a spin* on her busy little world at mealtimes.

"Sit down, finish your dinner, and start living a real life. This is fantasy," announced her father, more than once, worried about Little Leo and her intense new interest in boys. Where were the days when she made him make believe food in her toy kitchen and waited with serious concentration for his wide-eyed positive reassurance. Now she was borrowing all sorts of things from Billy. Makeup, wigs, and some performance style clothes had made their way into Little Leo's small bedroom. Her parents frowned at such *regalia* for a young daughter but knew better than to outright forbid it.

Both Mom and Dad, Louise (LouLou), and Harold, had done some pretty scary stuff when they were young and knew the road their daughter could take without some understanding and firm boundaries. They'd been raised in *single occupancy* hotels and motels, *lived rough* on the street when their parents were struggling in mind and body, and had only escaped by a *hair's breadth* themselves into a new world of parenting.

They both worked long hours, trading shifts to be home, at a furniture warehouse in the next town. The furniture came over on ships from Asia and trucks from Mexico, manufactured cheaply. They and many other workers rerouted smaller trucks to deliver goods around the two states and shared information about better and much worse places than their small part of Stockton.

The kids were turning out well, though just ahead lay the pressure all children get or take part in with their peers. Alwin seemed dismissive of crazy kids – as he called them. Little Leo however was being taken in completely by stories both real and imagined which young adults her age exchanged with the certainty of a fact. It was easier, they now now as parents, to follow the wrong person to the wrong place. Only Alwin with his old man's mind seemed ready to reject fantasy and trouble for a quiet safe place. He knew too much for a child of nine and this was a worry.

How Do I Get Out of Here

Miss Pascal drove her little red convertible at high speed to keep up with traffic on the busy interstate and get to the teacher's pre-semester meeting at the small school she worked at in Stockton. Her commute was fortunately a bit longer than others. Fortunately, because Stockton was a risky place to be after dark and even a teacher beloved by the community could be in danger. She lived in Althorp just south of Stockton where she, her husband, and their two daughters were living up until now, in *relative comfort*.

Her husband had just *served her with divorce papers*. She'd keep the house and kids, but she'd have to do it on less than half the combined income she was used to. Devoted to her teaching job at a small charter school, she had to teach summers elsewhere to make a reasonable amount of money to cover her kids' expenses. Now, she'd found out her husband had left her for another woman and this woman was carrying her soon to be ex-husband's child. And her husband had charged up their credit cards and then quit his job. A divorce would mean she'd have to pay him.

Frida and Gloria, her two daughters, at ten and eleven were the wonder of her life. Told she'd never get pregnant both pregnancy announcements from her doctor were surprising and joyous. In those days, her husband was proud of his wife, and promised her everything. In retrospect, it should have been the warning. No one can give you everything you want and it's useless and *chancy* to think or plan on it.

***

This morning the girls had been arguing over what they *perceived* their father's actions were and why he'd done this to them. Miss Pascal had allowed them to run free with their thoughts hoping to catch what they really thought about the change in their life.

"Hey little girl," Gloria chided her younger sister. "Papa loves us and he's still gonna be our father. Right mom?" Miss Pascal shrugged.

"And which one of us lives with him and who stays with mom," the older girl asked.

"Nitwit, dad doesn't want us anymore. it's just us women taking on the world when we haven't even asked for it" Frida replied. The protective younger sister wrapped her thick dark arms around her older sister who stood there in disbelief, ready to burst into tears. Gloria had been closer to her father as both were athletic and competitive in soccer, lacrosse, and tennis. Her father had coached her from the first day Gloria said she wanted to be like Serena and Venus. She wanted to conquer the world with something she enjoyed doing.

Frida understood her sister's unhappiness, grateful also that she was the one who looked after her mother, as she saw it. Her mom's students had difficult lives and she often told her girls to be appreciative of what they had and understand *privilege* was a fragile thing. Her mom would get so down from the condition her students lived in up in Stockton, but she also admired them for their strength and commitment to show up at school almost every day, clean, well-dressed, and ready to get on with their education.

***

Pressing the accelerator, Miss Pascal roared north up Interstate I-5 ready to take on the day. Today, meant signing the girls into the high school division of the charter school she taught at. It would hurt at first, but it was better than having to sell the house. This option would only mean trying to find a more expensive home in the already overpriced town. The girls would miss their school, but they could stay in the *park and rec* organization they both knew and loved. Gloria, for her tennis, and Frida for the outstanding arts program; they were both happy and involved. Each program boasted winners and graduates who grew to be exceptional in their adult development. This program would balance the change of schools and as it was, her charter school was a highly regarded and lauded school for *young people's evolution.*

It was for the best, she tried to reason, how her husband left at this point in their daughters' lives. Any younger and they would feel abandoned, unsafe, and unloved. Enough had happened in their own community and schools that the two young girls understood relationships might not last forever. Their close ages had been a benefit as often they were more like twins, liking the same pop stars, clothes, and foods. Resilience, however, was a very different story. Frida, the younger sister, was *rational,* practical, and flexible and calm when it came to problems. Gloria on the other hand was over reactive, *literally minded,* and *fixated* on things she could not easily understand. They balanced each other well and Miss Pascal had no serious worries about them. Well, except they were both about to make a huge change in schools and friends.

What a Relief

Billy again paced his small place after Alwin passed on the message from the men. They needed him to do something was all they said. Later, cleaning at the motel, then filling in for a friend at city hall janitorial, Billy could not stop thinking about his finding the treasure and the probable cause for the men's request. If they knew what he had, it would not have been a request. It might have been a bullet. Still, in this town, everyone watched each other, and made use of the information. Plus, he didn't want Alwin caught up in this. He was a great kid, so much smarter than anyone realized. Hey, maybe Alwin already knew. Billy shook his big bald head, *confounded* those kids knew more about everyday events than adults who might be trying to block out the world around them, if it was bad news.

Billy stopped by the car repair joint that *stripped cars* from around the county and resold the parts to many small shops. Some of the cars were stolen. Well, probably most of them.

"Whoa, Marquesa do a turn for us!" The workmen all stopped to hoot and whistle at the tall, burly, part-time performer. "Estavio is in the back, Marquesa. He wants to see you now."

The Dark Afternoon

Alwin heard them when the car was still far away. The small bright-blue, souped-up car made so much screeching engine/tire/brake noise and the thin tattooed arms hanging out the windows meant there were no serious adults inside, he sensed. He was correct. The powerful stereo in the car announced the beginning of something bad.

***

Loulou ran into the Emergency Room at the brand-new County Hospital. Little Leo had called her on the payphone, sobbing and telling her to come to the hospital quick. Fast! Now! Her mother tried to calm her down and demanded to know if Alwin was okay but Little Leo had already slammed the pay phone receiver into the hook.

When she arrived after a deeply scary drive across town, the ER waiting room was crowded with people as always but this time, something was different. All of them were crying. Many nurses, *maneuvered* around the room, questioning, and comforting those who appeared to be uninjured. She did not see her son or daughter and a massive, yet invisible, angry hand gripped her heart. The noise was unbearable and the nurses at the desk, surrounded by police officers with walkie talkies were all busy with the throng of people demanding information.

Loulou ran around the room searching for her two kids, noticing how many people had blood on their clothes, faces, and arms. She began to sob *alternating* with hiccups and still found neither of her children. She ran down the hall towards the cafeteria and there was Leontine, her little face pressed against the wall, the phone planted at her ear. She was talking to someone about shots! Shots! Shots!

Loulou grabbed her by her small thin shoulders and spun her around. Dropping to her knees she hugged her daughter with a relieved *desperation*. Little Leo stopped talking and stared at her mother in shock. Her eyes were bubbly with tears and snot ran down to her lips. Her mouth was open in a silent plea, and she nestled her face into her mother's soft, warm neck.

"For God's sake, Leo! Where is Alwin? Where is your brother? Tell me little girl, where is he?" Leontine searched around the hall groggily crazed again in a new panic, then pulled her mother into the cafeteria. Starting to *bawl again*, she pointed to Alwin sitting with a group of other children *dolefully* eating ice cream cones. Alwin saw his mother and waved weakly, a blank expression on his face. The small boy was in shock.

"Oh, thank God! Oh, thank you, Jesus!" Loulou dragged her still clinging daughter over to Alwin and placed her other arm around him. Once again, she dropped to her knees beside both of her very precious children.

She stared silently into the little boy's face, looking for an emotion and found none. He looked back at her eyes, silently, continuing to nibble on his ice cream cone, the cool cream drippings running onto his small chubby hand. He shook his head *benignly*, then looked away from his mother.

***

Later, Billy marched over to the front house from his garage apartment. By now everyone had heard about the playground. Billy guessed why it had happened and he was most likely the cause of it. Late at night, last week, he had found the money in the alley, by taking a short cut to get home quickly from cleaning rooms, without attracting attention. Just to the side of a broken-down garage, leaning badly, sat a neatly wrapped package. What was something in waxed shipping paper doing in a dirty, dark alley filled with garbage? He took it quickly,

103

putting it in his duffel bag, and looked around anxiously to be sure he had not been seen. After *darting* home completely in the shadows, Billy partially opened the package. He was blown away by the contents of the carefully unwrapped parcel. It was almost $100,000 in cash, all $100 Franklins. And no one knew he had it.

Estavio had not guessed it was Marquesa, proven, as he had asked Marquesa earlier to watch everything and everybody. He was missing something and all he would tell Billy was it was his and it was valuable. "Just keep an eye on everyone, ok? Let me know what stuff changes. You're one of us. You know what I mean." Estavio spoke gently but with frightening authority.

Relieved by the unexpectedly positive meeting outcome with Estavio, Billy lived for another day. But now Marquesa had brought trouble and death to the children. And all of them were dear to Billy. How would he get out of town? He pondered the package when he returned home before he talked to the family he was closest to, literally and *figuratively*.

A Plan For Now

Miss Pascal sat at the end of the table where the grade schoolteachers faced the administrators and high school teachers across a triangle formation. It would be a different meeting for her this time.

"Alright, welcome back, everyone," the well-dressed female Director said softly. "Before we start talking about our summer, we should first address the shooting at Summers Park. It will mean our children are going to be in shock, will need more patience and, as always, look to us for a stable and let me emphasize this, a safe place to thrive."

After sharing what they knew and felt, the meeting became more about business subjects. The discussion went on with introductions for new faculty and outlining some changes in schedule due to Talk Time. Talk Time would be one period just after lunch, when Core Curriculum, lunch and recess had finished for the day and before they jumped into Physical Education and Art Classes. They couldn't give it as much time as it needed but they had State and Federal *mandates* to fulfill again this year. The idea was to just let the children ask questions of any type and answer these as best the teachers and school psychologist could.

Miss Pascal opened her wallet to stare at pictures of her two daughters. Beautiful girls, the loves of her life, she hoped she was making a good decision for them. They had visited the school when they were younger and spoke judgmentally about the differences between this, a center city school, and the beautiful private school they thought they were going to continue attending. Her part was easier she realized. She snapped her worn wallet crammed with credit cards closed and resolved to do the best for them. It was going to be a tough year in so many ways.

"Any last items for discussion before we head into program schedules," the Principal inquired softly.

Miss Pascal raised her hand and when called on announced, "my husband has served me with divorce papers and I will be enrolling my daughters here, today. Thank you for your support and patience in advance."

No one spoke for a moment, some *mouthed "sorry"* to her but a few teachers and admins cast *condescending* glances at her. "My the mighty had fallen," Miss Pascal could guess they were saying in their Inner Voice.

Inner and Outer Voice was a traditional practice in the school to reduce conflict. Outer Voice was what you wanted people to know, and Inner Voice was how you really felt. Part of the school's programs like all others around the country were introducing *Cognitive Behavioral* and *Mindful* practices to the students and staff. Those who did not pity her today also mocked this program. These people had grown up in dangerous places and *"an eye for an eye"* was still part of their mindset. Who said adults play fairer than kids?

The Ride Back

Jupiter grabbed the "shotgun' seat in the front on the way back from Las Vegas. It was his uncle's truck and Renny didn't mind at all. He wanted to stretch out in the back to think on some important upcoming people and places. When he got back to school, he would see Little Leo again. He missed her and her bragging, confident ways. Uncertain if they were going steady or just friends, Renny did not know how far to push or be playful. Shy as he was and still very awkward, he was drawn to the brave, intelligent, and energetic girl. And there were other things he had to think about. Yeah, the thing.

"Hey bro," Jupiter slapped the headrest without turning around to Renny and began to giggle. "I know what you're thinking about man. You probably got your whole head doing the business of school and some people you can't wait to see, huh? My man is still making moves in all directions, huh? Must be tough to figure out your mess. I'm here for you, man." Jupiter looked back at his best friend, winked, and nodded. "I promise; no matter what happens, bro."

The ride took forever and within a short time both the boys drifted off to sleep. Snoring almost in unison. Jupiter's uncle welcomed the peace and quiet.

Homecoming

Racca and Anjelah had called each other as soon as they heard about the shooting. They were both shocked and grief stricken but so relieved their boys had been elsewhere. It could have happened to them. The central park was a natural hangout for kids from three different neighborhoods and it resembled a *middle eastern bazaar* with kids mingling, other kids playing b-ball, hopscotch, and just showing off. Many of the kids *promenaded*, not aware promenading was a practice through the centuries.

See and be seen. Most parents allowed their kids to go to parks because the old people sat guard on benches around the play areas sharing their own stories, gossip, and playing cards. It would never be the same again. The loss of social public gatherings would spread around the United States and the world. In time, only protesters would dare to join together, where to no one's surprise, they would be tear gassed and beaten by the authorities.

***

Both Jupiter and Renny were surprised by the emotional welcome their moms gave them, hugging, kissing, and saying such sweet things in different gentle languages. Jupiter's solemn grandmother with her rosary in hand moaned prayers over her grandson's head, kissing his thick hair again and again as she prayed. He

107

sat confused while his mother smiled at him with quiet joy. Grandmother intoned in whispers for the adjustments they had made and suffered by coming to *Estados Unidos*, losing some family in the horrible and illegal passage, and now ending up in just as dangerous a place.

As soon has he possibly could, Jupiter placed a frantic call to Renny. Jupiter shared some of what his grandmother had said in Spanish. "Man, she said little kids died along with some grandpapas and grandmamas. They still haven't said how many. Who do you think it was?" He stopped short knowing he and Renny had good friends and family in the community. What if it had been one or more of them?

After they finished, Renny hung-up the phone with a sick feeling in his stomach. He was going to see Little Leo, right now. When his mother refused him permission and demanded he remain inside, he agreed, and then ducked out his bedroom window and slid down the sad tree to the ground. Taking off like a racehorse he got to her house in record time. Literally, there had been no one on the streets. No cars, no people, and no cops to see him or stop him. It was freaky.

Loulou was startled by the knock on their door. She peeked through a window curtain and could not see anyone there. Renny, almost invisible, was leaning against the opposite side of the front door suddenly realizing he wasn't ready to hear or accept that Leo might be one of the dead. He was shocked and scared by this *probability*. He had been prepared for years that Little Leo might reject him for so many reasons she had but knowing she might be gone, even now, made him bust into soft desperate tears.

Loulou decided not to open the door. She did not even ask who it was, afraid it was a trick, and she was all alone with her kids still in shock.

Alwin and Little Leo were in their beds, pretending to read, but thinking about the scene at the park. The noise. The screaming. The shots just kept coming.

Little Leo wiped her tears away and slid down from her bunk and into Alwin's. She wrapped her long arms around Alwin, trying belatedly to protect him, and claim his sense of calm as her own. Alwin folded himself into his big sister's arms feeling guilty he had ever questioned her, dragged her back to seriousness, or dismissed her vivid fantasies. He'd do better with her, he promised himself.

***

Renny stood outside in the dry, hot, darkening night. He was uncertain if he should bang on the door which might attract attention and scare people. No answer meant they weren't home he theorized. What if it had been Leo or her brother, or horribly both. The park and their home were the only places he could count on their appearance. This was too hard for him. He was sure they were dead. He shivered and hugged himself tightly allowing long held tears and unhappiness to flow from his body. He wasn't ready for this. It wasn't fair to them. Convinced it was worse than possible, Renny decided to sneak quietly back home where all was not well either.

***

Anjelah was pacing the kitchen. Her candles were lit, she had placed flowers around the table for those who had died and for those who must mourn for their children. Needing to reassure herself Renny was safe she had knocked on

109

her son's bedroom door. Receiving no answer, she entered the room. He wasn't there and the window was open. She knew exactly what he had done. That girl. He was going to check on her. "Don't be a stupid hero, my baby" she moaned in Vietnamese. She heard the front door open and close softly.

Renny came to his bedroom door, surprised to see his mother hunched on his bed looking unusually old and tired. She glanced at him quickly and patted the bed next to her. He sat. Anjelah wrapped her arms around her boy, almost a man, taller than she was and so smart her heart twisted and struggled with pride and fear. "Please, don't let anything happen to my son," she pleaded silently.

***

Racca was not so calm over the next several days. School was starting soon and the playground where controlled drop-off and pickups were handled would be even more heavily guarded. More safety protocols would be put in place, and she would be required to pick Jupiter up in person. And only bad parents would let their kids walk to school alone, she thought. How was she going to work? Her ancient mother would have to do it. She would finally have to leave the house to support her daughter and grandson. This might take many miracles. Racca looked heavenward making a direct plea.

Decision, Decisions, Decisions

Billy was frantic. It was only a matter of time he thought. Sooner or later Estavio would start taking hostages, making threats, and the little community would turn on each other to protect themselves. They wouldn't even have to know anything; just make up stories and lies to keep their own health. If Billy left, they would find him. Maybe they knew about his ex-wife and kids. Big money meant big fast efforts to hunt the thieves. They would hurt Loulou, Harold, and the kids without hesitation for information. He needed to do something and quickly before the screws tightened.

***

Renny also paced his room through the following days, promising his mother he would not leave their home without permission again. He had been calling Little Leo's house, but no one picked up. Ever. He heard on the radio the cops were not releasing the names of the people hurt or killed while the investigation was underway. The community was silent and even good neighbors did not make eye contact. They did not know who had been involved and until they did, they would all stay *under the radar*. For having worked so hard for so little in life, still they felt they all had too much to lose.

How was Renny going to find out? He called Jupiter several times a day, and his friend meaning to calm Renny, asked him questions about his family to divert his friend's fear and anxiety. Jupiter knew so little about the tiny Vietnamese family. Anjelah and her son were the most private people anyone knew. They gave away nothing about their past or present except Renny's dad had been Black. "Where had he gone," Jupiter asked politely.

This quiet questioning worked *momentarily* as Renny opened up about what he knew which was so very little. His mom meant to protect him. When he was small, she told him his dad was a soldier who was serving a long stint. As he got older, Renny questioned why his father did not send letters or presents to his family, or even a little money. Was there a bigger problem?

His mother changed her tactics and used other excuses. Renny could pick among her reasons for an absent father though somehow, he knew she had not offered the truth at any time. He challenged each one of her reasons, and she put him off, sometimes angry, sometimes silent, and often simply dismissed his questions; telling her son he was better off never knowing. When was she going to start treating like an adult, or at least a kid with a good brain and common sense? Asking again and again only led to Anjelah's silence and refusal to meet his eye.

***

The next morning the motel manager told Billy a group of kids, probably college frat boys looking for a place to party had rented a room for the night, tore it apart, and left when his back was turned. "Would Billy help him change out the furniture today? Touch it up, small repairs?"

***

"Estavio there?" Billy asked when someone picked up the phone. "Hey yeah, Estavio, you have to come to Room 14 at the Wakefield. I was doing damage repair and I think this is what you're looking for." The line went dead, and Billy nervously continued to touch up the paint in Room 14, trashed by the young group who had split. They had paid cash, which the motel owner liked but now there was no chance to collect for damages.

It was just minutes before Estavio's black Benz screeched to a halt in the empty motel parking lot. Billy had timed his call to Estavio during the motel manager's lunch break. Billy looked after the desk in those very slow hours of the day from whatever room he was cleaning.

The man of great importance within their community stood silently at the door, dressed in black with spurs on his pointed toe boots. Billy *gestured* over to a cheap, wood board, battered desk. Estavio lifted it to see and there, duct taped to the underside of its single drawer was a package wrapped in the white shipping paper. One corner was cut open and the rest had been badly scotch taped. Billy had worn gloves for the opening, closing, and *transporting* the package to the room this morning after the manager's request call.

"Who?" demanded Estavio. Billy briefly explained a group of kids, paid cash, the signature was just a squiggle on the motel register, trashed the room, and split in the early morning hours when no one could see them. Typical customers.

Playing dumb, Billy asked, "what do you think? Why would they leave this behind?"

Estavio violently kicked and stomped the desk to pieces, grabbing the still-taped-to-the-drawer package. He took a long look at Billy, who *well-advisedly* just stared at the smashed desk, then Estavio hurried towards the door. Estavio looked back at Billy, "Marquesa, I owe you a big one. Be well."

Billy went back to touching up the paint, but his large trembling hands made many mistakes.

***

Renny had promised not to leave their home, but Jupiter had made no such promise. He wrote a note, folded it, attached some tape, and took a walk over to Little Leo's house. He didn't ring the doorbell or knock but walked around to the backyard. He placed the note with Leo's name facing inward on the window, he knew was over the kitchen sink. Pleased and giggling he walked back home, shuffling, thinking about better days ahead. He'd get them all out of here with some help.

***

Miss Pascal had finally called a lawyer. The woman was helpful and comforting. She had dealt with this before and she would make Miss Pascal's husband regret everything he had done. She was pleased the kids would be moving to a good school in a *blighted* neighborhood to save the home. It strengthened her case before the judge. And she swore to Miss Pascal that her kids would be back in private school within a year. Yes, it takes a long time, she assured the grateful mother and teacher, but the children's comfort and welfare would be a relatively quick matter. Details would take longer but the results would be improved by patience on Miss Pascal's part, and *relentless aggression* by the attorney.

After the call, Miss Pascal sat down with her daughters. This was the hard part, and it went reasonably well if she balanced out their completely surprising reactions.

Frida, usually the thoughtful one, literally screamed. And kept screaming for a long time without pausing for a breath. She was adamant she was not leaving

114

her school; she was not giving up her friends, she was not going to "that place".

Even the usually overreactive, stressed out Gloria was shocked at her sister's reaction. Frida was usually the rock, the immovable calm stone. She could talk her older sister into better behavior and out of the craziness Gloria experienced internally. "What is up with you, little sister?" Gloria chided the younger one.

Frida, now in a complete rage even as she sat at their kitchen table, smacking her hand on the table to mark each one of her statements, continued in a growl.

"I'm not going." Smack!

"Why is he doing this?" Smack!

"What did you do to him?" She growled at her mother. Smack!

"I am too young for this treatment!" Smack!

And what followed was a commanding speech filled with surprising obscenities and harsh words for them all. Miss Pascal and Gloria stared at each other, then at this little person they both thought they knew.

Usually, the girls' parents allowed them to yell and argue, or negotiate if needed, without interruption. Trying to stop a meltdown midway never went well and eventually the children, tired and worn out, would lapse into silence and some sort of temporary calm. This moment of Frida's however was a *magnitude greater* than their family had ever experienced before and not from the sister they expected. They would have laughed if the tirade was not about an important challenge for their family.

Frida's rage shocked Gloria into a slightly better mood and perspective on their parents' problems. When Miss Pascal reiterated the lawyer's promise that everything would return to something near normal and the change of schools would only be temporary, Gloria looked at her sister with a silly toothy smile and thumbs up meant to reassure her little sister.

Frida was not having it. Her eyes narrowed as she took in her mother and sister's comical attempts to stop a lava flow. "I'm going to bed, (smack) and I will only come down for dinner (smack). I will not talk about this (smack) and I'm warning you, I'm in no mood to cooperate (smack). If my father calls, I'm going to speak to him (smack). Okay?" Friday stared at her mother as she lowered her chin to her chest, her eyes were slits, barely showing a gleam of the eyes behind them.

Gloria decided then it was going to be a tough year and she had better ramp up her care for her little sister and *reclaim* her own common sense. Her own supply of comfort was limited to just her mother now. She was planning to be a wonderful big sister though she didn't realize she would be bitten many times in the process. There would be some other things Frida belly-laughed about a decade later, trying to get her *nonplussed* big sister to join in the good-natured laughter.

A Quiet Storm Spreads

The neighbors had almost completely stopped speaking to each other. The relationships that normally stood through good and bad times were beginning to fall apart. The mass shooting of innocent children, the first of any kind in their crime-filled community was a precedent. It meant the usual rules of behavior were gone. Despite the young men and one woman who were in the car being caught

116

and placed in the county jail away from older prisoners, information leaked out how the shots had come from several directions. Were people in various groups shooting at each other under cover of the usually normal playground? Was this gang related or a massive cooperative event?

Either way, parents already struggling before the shooting, were beginning to make efforts to leave quickly. Many were *resorting* to unusual strategies to make this happen. Others were bewildered by the necessity of finding a safer place which would accept them.

***

Racca pondered a move over and over in her mind without at first telling Jupiter. Jupiter, on his own, had told her how much better Las Vegas would be for them. They had family, there were jobs, and inexpensive, safer housing. Why wait?

Racca had responded too quickly. She wanted time to plan a move and she threw the first thing she could back at her son's common sense. "So big boy, you're not going to miss Renny and your other friends? Ready to just jump and go?" Unfair! Mother and son knew it and Racca could not forgive herself for *inadvertently emotionally blackmailing* her beloved child.

Jupiter was loyal and *caring to a fault*. He could talk anyone of them out from a dark place. His positivity and unselfish concern for others was *lauded* among family and at school. The teachers there were filled with praise for Jupiter. He could take any idea and reduce it to its essential points. Children responded well to his leadership in a calm indirect way, lining up with whatever cause he was

117

supporting. His mother's fatigue and desperation were taking a toll on her committed love to her family.

More than a decade ago, Racca had crossed the border at night with only two others. Large groups drew the attention of the Border Agents. Warning shots could hit a human target, especially if the target was truly desperate and just kept going. Her little group, three strangers, made it by pausing and running again and again in explosive patterns. Luck and love were truly with them on their travel day. Her cousin Connie had left for the States the night before and was never seen again.

She made the *sign of the cross* over her chest. Maybe it was time to run again. She had more support this time. Jupiter was smart and it took a lot to get him to panic. He was growing up and maybe she should *acknowledge* this.

Racca settled on the sofa, squishing herself in next to her son, who bored, was watching *telenovelas* with his grandmother. She allowed him to move his *hefty* legs across her much smaller lap. She stroked the boy's legs, he who had been such a wonderful little baby. He had never cried and she and the family worried that he might be *challenged*. Tio, her brother offered how maybe the baby was *retarded*, a word never used today except by angry little children to one another. He wasn't. Jupiter, Eduardo Alphonse Jesus Dominic, as he was baptized, was taking it all in. Learning, watching, and getting far ahead of all the children and many of the adults.

When he was 13-months old, his first words ever directed to his mother were, "no carrots now. I want fruit." Racca, her mother, and the others in their small kitchen froze. Then they laughed, which caused little Jupiter to stare angrily at

118

all of them. "Is this what you want my little love?" Racca asked her *miffed* toddler The adults were shocked again when Jupiter answered in mixed Spanish and English. "Mama, I'm hungry. No funny me!"

***

Gloria could not sleep that night as Frida tossed and turned in her bed, talking aloud and mumbling words of defiance. The elder sister was relieved when Frida rose slowly from her bed, tossed the blankets aside and shuffled out of the bedroom. A bathroom break was just what her sister needed. Maybe she was going down to the fridge, hungry from her determined hunger strike during dinner earlier, her arms crossed refusing everything but a bit of lettuce.

Her mother shook her awake. "Gloria, where's your sister? The front door was wide open! Where is she?" Gloria sat bolt upright; eyes still sandy but wide open. It took her a few seconds to comprehend what her mother was saying. They both rushed down the stairs to the front door. Miss Pascal had closed it, but reaching it first, Gloria flung it back open. On their small front patch of grass stood Frida. Standing completely still, staring at the house, Frida made no move. Mother and sister rushed to her, and she did nothing in response. Miss Pascal shushed Gloria, putting both arms around the younger daughter.

"Frida, can you hear me? Frida, why are you out here? Honey, we must go back inside." Slowly the two pushed and pulled Frida back to the house. Guiding her to her bed, Gloria helped her mother remove Frida's pajama onesie. It was torn a bit at the shoulders. The knees were grass stained, and they were horrified to see the feet of pajamas were blackened, with garbage debris, bits of earthen mud, and

119

something smelling horribly stuck to them. None of this came from the front lawn or even their street. Where had the sleepwalking Frida gone? The streets all around here were *immaculate*.

Maybe For Now

Billy had signed on again with a few bars in Sacramento for night work, and at the Holiday Inn as a full-time janitor and a room cleaner when needed. He could not leave here now. Not for some time. And for the first time, Loulou and Harold, asked Billy, *pointedly* not Marquesa, to look after their children when their shifts overlapped. An hour here and there. Billy understood the parents trusted him now though they really had no choice. They devised a system of signals and codes designed to communicate without startling the children.It was difficult for Billy. He loved these children as his own. He had brought this disaster on the community and each day he could see how Leo and Alwin had been profoundly changed by the shooting. He spoke gently with both during these short interactions trying to be positive and supportive, drawing them to subjects he thought would make them laugh.

One day it happened unexpectedly. He was desperate for material to engage the two sad children. Half dozing, he started to talk about some of his funnier experiences on the drag circuit. Both children stopped and *took stock* of the man before them, They'd seen Marquesa wrapped in glitter and bangles head out in her car. They knew what he did. Now, he was letting them in on an adult's experience. Good stuff!

The stories were about missteps and small troubles in Marquesa's work with voices and moves supplied theatrically by Billy. Then it happened. Both children began to giggle, looking to each for tentative reassurance, then bursting out in laughter. First Alwin, then Little Leo, stood and began to *pantomime* moves from Billy's dialogue.

The three were interrupted by Harold's quiet entrance. Taken by surprise, the three froze. Harold paused for only a second, then scooped his children into his arms. "Keep going, keep going," their father pled. Soon the four were dancing happily with each other to an old disco song from the radio. Harold dried his tears as he turned up the music.

***

Jupiter was careful to engage Renny carefully when they were alone. He did not know what his forged letter had done or if Little Leo had even received it. He had been careful knowing there was a good chance the girl's parents would find the letter first. Nothing *objectionable*. Just concern, a show of affection, and the hope Renny would see her soon at school. The letter expressed concern for her whole family but was directed at Leo exactly as Renny would have expressed himself. He knew his friend well, *aping* his handwriting and his speech patterns was easy.

***

"Hey bro! My mom thinks we can get to Vegas in a few months. She did say it might take a year though. And listen, my family wants your family to come with us. My mom is going to talk to yours. Maybe she did already? What's going on,

121

man? Why are you so quiet?" Jupiter, so happy about this change of events and the inclusion of his best friend, was puzzled by Renny's quiet.

After a minute, Renny began to speak. His words were carefully chosen, and he hesitated to *formulate* each sentence perfectly. He had no intention of hurting Jupiter, yet there were, as always, complications. An invitation, which Racca had offered Anjelah, was on the table. When his mother told him, he was torn, and as usual his anxiety increased. It was like too many planes coming in at once and people's lives at stake. It was up to him, Anjelah had announced, stay, or go, be ready with a moment's notice? Could mother and son understand what this change would mean for both?

***

Miss Pascal shared breakfast with Frida as Gloria was frantically tearing her closet apart. This was their last leisurely breakfast before school started tomorrow. Gloria needed the perfect clothes and Frida needed to know what she had done. It wasn't her fault, nor mother or daughter's, but Frida should know what took place. Yet, her mother wasn't sure. Parenting is not an easy thing.

Gloria and her mother had agreed to *surreptitiously* place objects, such as chairs and stacks of noisy things around Frida's bed and in front of the bedroom door. In the days before this morning, there appeared to be no other sleepwalking events. Gloria and her mother had not slept well but it was *essential* they watched Frida carefully. The condition of Frida's pajama feet from that disconcerting night had made them both nervous and uneasy.

122

"Honey, do you know what happened the other night?" Miss Pascal *queried* her youngest. Frida remained much less verbal and accommodating after her meltdown. She stared back at her mother as she spooned oatmeal with nuts and fruit, her favorite, *deftly* into her mouth.

"Sweetie, you took a long walk in the middle of the night in your pajamas. You seemed to be asleep the whole time, even after we found you. And it seems," here her mother paused to hold back tears, "you walked far from this neighborhood. Do you remember anything at all? Gloria and I found you on the front lawn. Honey, you went far away. We know this. Does it make sense to you?"

Frida, unusually for her, suppressing all emotion, responded to her mother quietly and succinctly. Thinking about how much or how little she wanted to share with her family, she paused, still chewing. Then carefully, without looking at her mother, she started.

" I had a dream, and I still can't understand it. In it, I was outside at night. I was walking and I couldn't find my way home. I thought if I went back to sleep, I would be home, like in a dream. I wasn't afraid. At first, I wanted to be away from here, and I wasn't scared. Then something changed, and I needed to be back in my bed fast. Now, I remember you and Gloria holding me on the lawn. In my dream, I went back to sleep and woke up in the morning. But then I got really scared. I wasn't wearing my jams, there were books and plates on the floor, a chair in front of our door. I thought I was trapped in a dream. I'm still in the dream, right?"

"No honey, you're all right now. This isn't a dream, and that night WAS a dream. But honey, you went somewhere. Not just around the neighborhood.

123

You're okay now, right?" Miss Pascal looked hopefully at her daughter, her arm around the child, and kissed Frida's warm *temple.*

Armor Up, We Are Off

The first day of school had come. Little Leo, Alwin, Frida, Gloria, Renny, Jupiter, and Miss Pascal each checked their look in the mirror. They had had their haircuts, their showers, and spent so much time picking the clothes they were wearing now. This gave them some confidence and pushed the anxieties they had all been feeling, backward into a quiet place of their minds. Each one took a deep breath, then resumed preparations.

The parents also took a long deep sigh, squared their shoulders, and got everyone to the school's front gate on a hot, sunny morning. Was this going to make their community, their families, and questions better or easier?

The End – Story One

Amira Ding Dong

Manhattan, New York - 2000

Introduction

Theirs was an upper-east-side of Manhattan, New York City, mixed-race family. The year is 2000. The parents, Alianna Khoumoun-Fletcher and Stanley Fletcher are divorced but remain good friends. Amira is the younger of their two children. She attends a private school, Reese Academy where her mother, a once famous author in Egypt, teaches to pay Amira's tuition. Her father, an American stockbroker, meets Amira once every other week for lunch. Though he's generous it's apparent Stanley is not comfortable as a parent. Amira's elegant mother is proud, stylish, and works strenuously to keep hers and the children's lives fulfilled and robust. "No time for *self-absorption*," she says.

The other residents of their building, adults, and children, in a formerly posh building now subdivided, and the staff, provide background for Amira's experiences.

Her classmates can't get a read on her. She is mostly *ornery*, somewhat an *introvert*. Her friends are "people who get her." The teachers though praising her work, focus more on star pupils. These stars often suffer from their parents' ambitions.

Her 17-year-old brother Monti is *severely autistic*, physically disabled, and bedridden. He is cared for by round-the-clock attendants who are not noteworthy except for Mr. Robinson, an older Black male former athletic coach, and Mrs. May, who hails from the Caribbean.

Monti only speaks two words: Dingdong and Puddin. Monti shows love and excitement when his mother and sister are present by shaking his whole body excitedly. Amira daily confides to Monti, reading, and sharing her day with him. He is her only true confidant and she alone believes he understands what she is going through.

Ultimately, the story shows Amira's evolution and maturation as she, Mr. Robinson and Mrs. May solve the riddle – why does Monti say, "Ding Dong?"

Leaving school each day

"Aaghh, I hate that place! School is horrible. I can't wait till I finish here. I may never go to another school after I'm sixteen. They can't make you, you know. Not after sixteen." Amira pulled her stretchy black headband off, and long waves of magnificent dark brown curly hair sprang free to form a soft bobbing halo around her pinched, angry, brown face.

The Telford twins both giggled knowing Amira so well. They knew each morning she was at school way too early to work on some project or get extra attention from her teachers and school administrators. Amira was smart, it was true, and she worked hard for her grades. She was never satisfied, however. This was a trap she built for herself, and she knew it, taking secret pride in her extra efforts.

The Telford twins met Amira on the first day of pre-K in the basement of Reeves Academy on the Upper East Side of Manhattan six years ago. Neither boy,

Axel nor Alex, could keep their hands off her glorious hair then. Their blonde crewcuts did not have the same fascination for Amira, but she gamely let them stroke the thick braid running down her back if their hands were clean. Boys! Stupid boys! The twin boys were in silent awe during these childish adorations and old Miss Oderbeier kept an uneasy eye on the young trio.

The Family

"Your beauty *portends* you will be important, well beloved, and you will make great changes in the world, *mademoiselle*. You are meant to do significant things. Your busy youth will not let you slow down to understand and enjoy these *privileges*. Look, take time, and let the world move around you playfully. For now, you must only observe."

The magnificent old lady, dressed beautifully in black silk from neck to toe, gripped her ivory-headed ebony walking stick harder, displaying her diamond ring covered fingers even more *prominently*. Amira stared into the woman's deep gray unblinking eyes, set in a *ravishing* olive-skinned *chiseled face*. It was too hard to meet the woman's steely gaze for long and Amira shifted her eyes to study the gems on her great aunt's fingers.

"Yes, my dear. These are the rewards of beauty. You, mademoiselle, would not think me beautiful now, but once, I had many choices. Potential husbands and their families promised me anything I wanted. I could choose from among these men my parents already approved of. You too will have these opportunities very soon. I know this for certain." Aunt Fazha turned her head *imperceptibly* to the photographer begging to get the two women into one portrait.

They *complied* and a dozen photos were taken of the regal white-haired woman, seated in her straight back chair and the young woman standing deferentially at her side. The family parties at Amira's cousin's house on *Beekman Place* were interesting and surprisingly for Amira, stress free. Here she learned who her mother's family really was.

The Egyptian *business coalition* was having important meetings with their ambassador in America, Amira's great uncle Mirtan, Aunt Fazha's husband in Washington DC. There were many extravagant parties and meetings attended by most of the Egyptian delegation. They would meet with the American Vice-President later this week. Aunt Fazha claimed she was "*tres fatigue*," so terribly bored and "over it". In truth, she adored these events.

Later after a great feast in the massive dining room, Amira, her mother, and her father spoke little in the taxi on the way home. The extended family did not know Amira's parents were divorced, and they did not know how much Monti suffered or required care. This stressed her mother completely, but her father claimed this for his family. It was necessary. The Khouroum family was wealthy and powerful. And though this did not affect the four of them directly at this time, Amira's father insisted on solidarity for the future of his children and the dignity of his ex-wife.

One of Many Chats

"Then Aunt Fazha and I had our picture taken. She kind of scares me, but she is beautiful and says wonderful things. She thinks I'll make a successful marriage. Hah! Only if it's a boy who doesn't pick his nose or calls every day to talk about himself. I'm not fixing anyone else. I'm too busy trying to get ahead too. But of course, I'd do anything for you." Amira kissed her brother Monti, on the forehead as she curled her long frame next her brother on his bed. His eyes roamed the room without focus when he was awake. If she stopped talking for long, Monti, distressed, would move, agitated if she was not sharing and interacting with him.

"Any way, when you get older and the new physical trainer comes, we'll get you to meet the family, right?" Amira prayed for such improvements in her brother's abilities. She desperately wanted this to happen. Only she and her mother still believed the future could be better for Monti. He knew love. He had tantrums often but what could they expect from a poor trapped boy?

"So, now let me tell you about my new teacher and the awful things the other kids say about her. I'm embarrassed. The teachers don't come from good families like ours." This statement stung her as she remembered quickly how her mother taught to cover her tuition, and the whole school, especially Gudrun and her friends knew this and gave Amira attitude. Amira never told Monti about the way some of the snobs treated her, or the things they said to her, or what one wrote on her desk in black marker.

Her mother counseled her to remain aloof and above it all, allowing things to happen around her but not get dragged into their dramas. Alianna Khouroum-Fletcher, made everything look easy, and if she wasn't having fun, clowning and laughing with her children, she had only one other way of acting. It was to behave and interact beautifully and always far better than her surroundings.

Patient, and *distant* from the chaos around her, her mother intimidated the other teachers and most of the other parents by her calm, polite dismissiveness.

People stopped to stare at her on the street as she swept past in her large black *cashmere* cape coat, long black hair in exotic braids wrapped around her head, framing her face. It was the only coat Alianna owned now other than her ancient ski jacket from university days. She threw that jacket on when Monti, her son, was being carried to the hospital in an ambulance because of one of his many disabilities. Her mother made the most of the few things she owned these days.

It Is The Day for Lunch

Amira dressed quickly, frustrated because Monti's new day and night healthcare attendants were changing at the same time. Usually, one overlapped and helped train the new recruit. It was difficult at those changeovers, but she and her mother helped filled in. This was going to be a nightmare. They wouldn't know how Monti liked things; how he liked his blankets, how he liked soft voices that played with his sense of humor, making him gurgle happily. They couldn't know he liked Robin Hood to be read over and over unless he was angry with you. Then he pretended not to care and would not listen even if it was Ivanhoe or Gulliver's Travels. These new people wouldn't know any of this.

And Amira couldn't stay because today she had to lunch with her father at one of his clubs. Dress up, make conversation, and try to remember to ask him questions about his thoughts and days. Her mother had practiced this with Amira many times, and it was only when Amira understood she was expected to act like an adult she rose to the task. She loved a good challenge. There were many real-life questions she wanted to ask her father, but her mother had gently forbidden it. It would embarrass both to be asked or answered, her mother cautioned.

The city bus took forever, but Amira's usual plans were to get somewhere earlier than expected and always bring a book. The Telfords reminded her she should just chillout sometimes. Her teachers tried to be enthusiastic about her overwhelming enthusiasm and *borderline* pushiness. Still, she arrived at the club on time, and the *maitre'd* seated her with her father who had also just recently arrived in his favorite dining room having a dozen immense crystal chandeliers. On this gray, overcast Saturday afternoon, tall, blonde, Stanley Fletcher was dressed well in blue blazer and gray slacks though he perspired and was unusually fidgety.

The waiter approached *immediately,* with the club manager right behind him. Amira overhead, as the manager whispered too loudly, how her father was several months in arrears for his club dues and today, his purchases would require cash. Her father nodded grimly and ordered salads for both. Water for both father and daughter and no *cocktail* for him today, thank you.

Amira let this news pass for now and started chatting hopefully by asking her father if he could give her some grown-up advice. Stanley Fletcher nodded but only half listened. *Nevertheless,* he responded positively and with some warmth to her future plans. Warmer than his usual self, he wore a brittle smile and gave a few polite curt nods to other people around them.

Amira encouraged by his unusual cooperation, pushed ahead with some important questions. Her father was direct in his answers as always.

"Why can't the Khouroums know about our family?"

"They *disdain* (his words) weakness, *vulnerability*, and *disabilities*."

"Why don't we see the others like us at social functions?"

"If they exist, they are too embarrassed to show up."

"Should we be?"

"We do the best we can and it's important to me that you have all the advantages of the Khouroum family connections, no matter what."

"No matter what? You mean Monti?"

"Yes, my dear. They would turn their backs on you and your mother if they knew"

"Why me and Mother? Why not you? It's not our fault and Monti's a wonderful guy."

"You don't really know that for a fact, Amira. Don't romanticize your brother's movements. He's responding to your attention and physical presence only. Not to your daily gossip."

"Monti knows who I am, and he knows all about me. Why can't you believe me, Father?"

"I'm sorry Amira, I don't see how it's possible. He's been tested, god knows. They're experts. I know you love your brother, but he is *not present* in the same way you and I are right now at this minute."

Amira was stunned by her father's emphatic reality. She had one more question, no, two more questions for her father.

"Why are you in arrears on your club dues? And should Mother know about this?"

Physically, he *deflated* a bit in response. He poked some salad leaves on his plate before answering. He spoke slowly and with an attempted level of warmth and a lack of bravery very different than he ever had before.

"Amira, you're at a strange point in your life. You know more, and your curiosity grows. You can ask all the questions you want but even with the cold hard truth you won't understand, and this will lead to an infinity of questions and more misunderstanding. Can you understand this? I can answer you, but you won't appreciate the answers and it might leave you more frightened or less in control of your emotions if you make up the *context* of questions and the answers. Knowledge happens in time."

"Father, I <u>always</u> want to <u>always</u> ask questions. It's important to learn from people you love who are more experienced. Why can't you and I do this? What is this lunch for then?"

"Amira, if you continue to push you become rude. And truly, sometimes," he said squaring his shoulders, sitting up, and glancing around the beautifully lit dining room, "it's none of your business." He pulled his wallet out, dropped two twenty-dollar bills on the table and waved for the waiter. Lunch was over.

Back At Home

Mr. Robby, the tall *elegant* elderly doorman, greeted Amira cheerily as he opened the great front door for her. "Nice new people looking after Monti today. I like them both. Very efficient, they asked plenty of questions about use of the elevator, and the best route to Central Park. I like them quite a bit. Monti will be happy, and you and your mom can relax a bit, eh?"

Amira gave the doorman a big bright phony smile in return. He'd confirmed her fears about new people with Monti. Monti was never supposed to leave their apartment. The defibrillator, the restraints, safety blankets, and torso cage were used more often than they knew. This was going to be tough. Gritting her teeth, Amira intended to play the heavy and let Mother be the soft, pliant one. They'd managed this before.

She dropped her dark blue, school uniform jacket on the small worn sofa in their tiny living room, walking past the kitchen and the room she shared with her mother. Stepping into the crowd around Monti's door, Monti sang out loudly, "Dingdong, Dingdong!" The two new people cheered Monti on then introduced themselves to Amira. They insisted on calling her Miss Amira.

"Miss Amira, I'm Evelyn May. It's a pleasure to meet such a beautiful sister to a wonderful young man. I'll enjoy chatting with you when you have time in your busy schedule." Mrs. May was a *slight* Caribbean woman, with large brown eyes, and a *lilting* accent. Amira tried hard not to like her and her voice, but the young girl knew she already wanted to please this woman. And she loved how Mrs. May regarded Monti so well. The others hadn't been so kind.

"Miss Amira, I'm Henry Robinson. I was an athletic coach for two decades and now I help young men like your brother reach their full potential. I love my work and your brother is already letting me know he wants it HIS way. We'll see." The large, muscled Mr. Robinson winked at Amira and ran his hand along Monti's arm. Monti, erupted with what Amira knew was his "very happy" movement. He was drooling plenty which Amira and their mother took to be

134

smiling. They'd had plenty of time alone with Monti and both considered their perspective the most important and *knowledgeable*.

"Now, we're going to change his room around a bit. We'll take some of the shelves out, turn the bed to the window, and put things back as we need them. Everyone okay, with that?" They all looked at Alianna for approval and she nodded, her *composure* like a regal princess though she covered her mouth with her hand. Amira knew her mother was going to cry.

"Good, so let's give us some room, okay. The big man will be back on deck in just a few minutes." Amira and her mother withdrew from the room to the tiny galley kitchen where Alianna began to prepare a simple dinner. They heard the grunts which included Monti's, and the furniture moving about.

Later the five of them ate together in Monti's room as he slurped his bottle of carrot ginger soup. Mrs. May chuckled, telling them how Monti had grunted in time with theirs when each piece of furniture was shoved. "Our boy was helping us, and he is very aware. He's on top of things. You see this too?" Mrs. May exchanged approving glances with Alianna and Amira.

Success. Then Mrs. May took the night shift and Mr. Robinson went home to sleep before his work with Monti began the next day. Mother and daughter were exhausted from worry and fell into a deep sleep in their own twin beds filling the smaller windowless bedroom.

Who Are My Friends

Gudrun was up to no good, as always. The extremely tall girl whose hair matched the color of her pale white skin, with brilliant teeth so large they scared small babies, had not liked Amira since Pre-K. Amira found the towering, imposing girl unnerving but had no interest in improving an already dead and cold to the bone relationship. Amira had too much on her mind and her schedule. Too many goals and responsibilities had blinded her to any person who did not approach or understand her in a particular way. "It is all such a waste of time," Amira lamented with the Telfords.

Amira, if asked, could tell you little bits about her school friends including the Telford Twins, but beyond a small trustworthy group, her classmates did not really exist for her. And she didn't worry about it, most of the time. She wanted less drama not more. Sometime, someone told her how school was a vehicle not a destination. It was one of her many mantras when people and situations attempted to undermine her or her academic goals.

Axel and Alex Telford had pointed this out to Amira long ago, begging her to be more *amenable*. "Say something nice. Nod and smile in their direction. Compliment them. Ask them questions," they coached her. Not anymore, Amira decided. Her behavior was already in place, and she wasn't interested in changing and sucking up to people she did not care about. It wouldn't go well, she told the Telfords. Then she remembered to thank them for their advice and patience. Alex complimented on her *acknowledgment*. "See," they said, "you know how. You do. High five!"

136

"Do you two guys know how seriously difficult it is to have a conversation with twins. It's an argument in surround sound. You two should get a job together torturing people by asking them something. Do you ever disagree?" Amira gently chided them.

"Yes. No. Yes!!" And the Telfords let loose their biggest problem. They somewhat blamed Amira. It was the way she spoke to them, not individually but as a committee. This awareness had been fermenting for a few months, Axel confessed to Amira. He was tired of being a twin. Alex on the other hand was fearful of a split, not having his much-loved brother around constantly, not supporting each other always, and possibly being very, very lonely. "We would be invisible" Alex cried to Amira, clutching her jacketed arm like a small child. "He wants his own room," sniffed Alex, already believing his own good life was over. Finished. Many things were changing, and it was hard to understand it.

***

"I *loathe* your hair. It looks like a broom from a backward country." Gudrun taunted Amira. Gudrun knew she was attacking one of Amira's points of pride.

"Whoa, Goodie!" The other four identically dressed girls in Gudrun's posse stepped away in tandem from Gudrun. "Unfair, and totally unreal," one of the young women hissed at their maybe-soon-to be-ex-friend Gudrun. "Seriously Gudrun, you thought her hair was a good place to start? Wrong! Seriously, I'd give your arm Goodie to have hair like Amira's," giggled another. Gudrun did not back down.

"Hey, I'm born here, I'm an American and my grades are better," Amira scolded. Gudrun smirked. She had only wanted an emotional response. She could have as easily made fun of the pencil in Amira's hand. Amira was easy picking and Gudrun had a confirmed hit, with witnesses. Leave them bloodless and unbloodied, Gudrun's older brother had taught her.

Later the Telefords, reunited for a just a wee second begged Amira to tell them how the fight went and who had *struck* first. Gudrun scared almost everyone at the school and a few teachers ignored her after having a long *contentious* conflict with the assertive, strong-minded student.

"She struck first."

"But you walloped her with your best material, girl?"

"No, I was lame and taken prisoner. It was so stupid. I must find out where she plans to go to college and cross it off my list," Amira rolled her eyes dramatically and pushed up her sleeves faking bravery and mimicking a series of karate moves at the same time. "Maybe school in Egypt for me?! It could work. I've got family there. Ok, maybe today wasn't so bad. Of course, it wasn't. It was lame and stupid."

"Do you need a bandage, wittle girl," *provoked* Alex. "You'll be fine. Just try to make some friends who are strong and fight back okay? We won't be here to carry your dead body out of the fighting cage. We'll be hailing a cab." Both boys chuckled for their friend. It had not been a big thing. Big bad things didn't happen at Reeves Academy. The twins told everyone the drinking fountain water was laced with something to make the kids cooperative and polite. Rebellion!! Can we do it after I finish this essay? This would be the silly, boring, rallying cry at their inner-city private school, they joked.

Another Close Call

Vito, the large burly super and his tiny, sweet wife, Toni, checked in on Monti and the Fletcher family each day, sometimes more than once. The building's only *antiquated* elevator was large, beat up, and often, out of commission. The couple knew the young EMTs, and their stretchers were dependent on the elevator to get Monti down to the ambulance when he needed it. "Hopefully, not today, Monti. Please not today, our beautiful young friend," they prayed out loud in Russian. They breathed deeply when another morning passed without an emergency call during the night.

Amira and her mother had clued Mr. Robinson and Mrs. May into the many necessary trips each month to the ER. Both professionals asked concerned questions about what preceded these visits. Mother and daughter told them what they knew. Stress and changes in habit had caused a few of the problems. Also, Monti was allergic to several vegetables, and they never knew until he was having an incident. A weak heart could drop Monti into a coma, and it often looked as though he was just sleeping. Talking to him, even waking him up was one of the best ways they knew to assess the boy's daily balance.

***

Later the same week after school, Robby, the doorman, informed Amira with a big smile that at that very moment her brother was in *Central Park* with both caregivers. IMPOSSIBLE!

"No, it's true. They have a pretty good wheelchair, and he's headed to some sun, noise, and all the beauty of Central Park. I hope he has a great time." Robby pointed in the direction of the park entrance, as he juggled the door open for old *patrician* Doctor Phillips. Amira took off like lightening. This was never supposed to happen.

A sweaty, frantic 15-minutes later Amira came upon her mother, Mrs. May, and Mr. Robinson as they and Monti lazily reclined in the warm September sun outside the shade of a group of tall trees and just off the walk filled with determined afternoon runners in shorts and baseball caps. Monti, in a complex high tech wheelchair sat completely still with his eyes closed. The others waved Amira over. The young girl slowed as she felt stinging tears of relief welling up in her eyes.

Amira wouldn't let any of them see her cry. She had dreamed she'd be the one to take her dear brother to the park. In her mind, she saw the two of them throwing crackers to the geese in the pond and racing the wheelchair around the water, laughing together. She'd point everything out to Monti and tell him three times what such things were called. Her mother and father would be seated nearby on a bench, her father's arm around her happy, beautiful mother. Today was good but still not all she hoped for.

Amira dropped her book bag and coat and slumped down to sit on the grass at Monti's side. She took his large chubby hand in her smaller slender dark one. He made a contented noise and began to drool. He was doing better; Amira knew in her heart. Though her heart and stomach were still tight at this moment, she wished they could stay like this all day, maybe every day. The park was such a place, dreamy noisy, frantic, and though you could feel completely alone it welcomed everyone.

Amira started singing an Egyptian song in Old Arabic she had learned *phonetically* from her mother. Alianna sang this to both her children many troubled nights. It was a gentle song and her mother told her it was not merely a calming children's song, but one reminding us how good moments were fleeting, and one should enjoy these rare times. It seemed perfect right now. Alianna joined in happily singing low and harmoniously as Mrs. May and Mr. Johnson directed the performance with gentle hand movements and nods.

***

The wall phone rang as soon as the five of them had returned Monti, who dozed on and off, back into his hospital style bed. Still light outside, thanks to Mr. Robinson and Mrs. May's room rearrangement, Monti could now enjoy the sight of a too-tall skinny tree wedged in the tight space between two wings of their building. The two brick walls were barely ten feet apart and neighbors could see and hear everything just across the way. When in full leaf however, the tree blocked the next building from view. It was a little forest and Monti had happily noticed the change in his own little existence, turning his face to each of them, to see if they saw what he saw, when he wasn't asleep.

141

Because of the new rearrangement, the two caregivers had to struggle less to get around Monti and he could also enjoy the view. It was necessary however to walk around to the foot of the bed to see Monti now. His face was not completely visible from the door to his bedroom. This was no problem for any of them if Monti was happy.

***

"*Mon cheri*, intoned the deep elegant voice of Aunt Fazha, "you are just the princess I was trying to reach." Amira had grabbed the phone before it woke Monti. "Mon cheri, you must at once, throw on your best dress and come to Beekman Place. Your lovely mother should attend, and your father if he is free from work." A small party is forming, and I think you should meet one or two guests. It's too exciting for words. Let me speak to *Maman*."

Amira handed the phone to her patient mother. Alianna listened for a few moments and *demurred* at attending any party on such late notice. She protested again and again, shaking her head towards Amira. Aunt Fazha was charming and *relentless*.

"Yes, all right, Auntie. Amira and I will attend but just for a short time. We'll be there as soon as possible but do not wait dinner for us. Amira has school early in the morning. *Je t'aime*."

"Yes, let's do this quickly," Alianna said to Amira. "Just an hour. Your father will be pleased, and we can dine there."

***

The huge *lacquered* double doors were open to the next great room where a table was set with crystal, rare dishes, and heavy silver. As mother and daughter took in the sight, the family and a few new young men circled them in happy welcome. Embraces and kisses were exchanged all around. It was such a good party, Alianna and Amira stayed for almost three hours.

In a taxi on the way home later Alianna was stressed. "I'm so sorry my child. I had no idea it would be a such a long evening. Is your homework finished? I will write a note and speak to your teachers if you haven't completed everything. The young men are the eldest sons of *prominent* men well known to my grandparents and myself. They are quite nice, and their families are *'tres formidable'* she said in French as they, including Amira, had chatted all night in French. "You don't have to think about marriage now if you don't want to. These are merely meetings between the good families of Egypt to show off their children. You did wonderfully. I could not be prouder of you. I've done so little to educate you in our *gentil* ways."

Alianna stroked Amira's braided hair, wrapped in a formal style around the back of her head, as her daughter snuggled in her arms. The mother hoped for the best for her daughter. Perhaps it was asking for too much too early but her ex-husband's monthly cash transfers to her account had stopped. This was not so unusual as his money varied each month based on his investing *prowess*. Alianna knew something extraordinary was happening to the stock market. Something about computer companies. She couldn't fix this problem so she would put it aside in her mind. She focused her thoughts again strictly on her children's welfare.

The taxi stopped behind an ambulance, with flashing lights, parked at the curb of their building. Mother and daughter jumped out of the car in panic. They both knew somehow it would be their Monti. What was she thinking, going to a party after Monti had such an impossibly wonderful new day, Alianna blamed herself? Change was so difficult for him.

The elevator was out of order again. Alianna, usually so calm, banged on the sign with anger and fear. "Why tonight?" she pleaded. Amira had already begun to climb to the fourth floor taking the stairs two at a time. After kicking off her last pair of elegant shoes, Alianna too ran up the stairs, holding her skirt and coat up around her knees. She prayed again as she always did when these events took them down a dark tunnel.

She reached Amira already screaming for someone to open the door off the emergency stairwell. It was jammed and both women tried to pull the door open by its handle. Alianna thought to throw her weight against the metal door, but Amira pointed out the door opened out towards them. Such frightened strength they threw into banging on the door to get someone's attention.

Then the heavy metal door slammed outward, throwing both women against the opposing wall. *Straightaway*, a stretcher rolled out towards them, forcing the two women up four stairs to avoid being crushed. As soon as she could, Alianna threw herself on the stretcher to see her son yanking the sheet off the completely covered body. She had to know. She had to see her son!

She froze as did Amira, sliding away from the stretcher. After a pause, the EMTs replaced the sheet carefully over the body throwing a hard look at Alianna. It hadn't been Monti. It was old Dr. Phillips. Both women were stunned.

He didn't live on their floor. What was happening? The two stared at each hoping the other had an explanation. None. In panic they both lunged for the closed door, and it opened easily now. Their apartment door was wide open, and Mrs. Phillips was being escorted out by a *solicitous*, comforting Mrs. May. Mrs. May was murmuring soft words to the elderly lady but managed to throw Alianna and Amira a surprised wide-eyed look. Not Monti, then?

Running past the two older women, mother and daughter entered Monti's room. Unbelievably, wonderfully, gratefully, the boy was snoring hard; deeply asleep. It was a different snore from his usual night noises but maybe the day out tired him beyond his usual indoor day. They stood gratefully over him until Mrs. May returned.

"I took Mrs. Phillips down to Miss Hazel's on the floor below. She's nice, they're friends, and there's not a thing anyone can do for that poor woman now. He just sat down on your itty-bitty sofa and went to sleep. Forever! Probably better none of us should sit there for a day until you can get it cleaned up nice," Mrs. May whispered in her beautiful lilting voice. The Caribbean woman kept looking *superstitiously* at the sofa as she adjusted Monti's blankets the way he liked them.

"How was your evening out, ladies?" Mrs. May admired both their gowns. Neither could speak for a few minutes. Both just nodded and Alianna held Amira's hand to her own chest. The three continued to stare at Monti. "Well fine, don't tell this poor old woman about your gorgeous night out." Mrs. May sat down in her sleeping chair resentfully.

You're Too Poor To Be Here

Renaissance Literature and Culture Class was a difficult place for Amira. Gudrun and five other students sat around one large table in the vast library as Mr. Antoine led the lesson. He was a *passionate teacher* and demanded much of his students. The Renaissance period, literally meaning rebirth in French, was his passion. All that was good in this world, art, science, and humanity evolved during this time, he asserted.

"So, what you're saying Mr. Antoine, is: European countries started the Renaissance, and elsewhere, like in Africa, Egypt, and the Middle East, people lived in dirt and ignorance," queried Gudrun with a smirk in Amira's direction. "I mean, what could those regions have been like compared to the richness of Europe." Gudrun thought she had stung Amira again.

"*Non, non,*" Mr. Antoine declared in French. "The cultures of these regions were far richer, far older, and far more developed than those in Europe. Africa was the originator of democracy, art, and medicine. It is by far the most exciting of all cultures and sadly, far less studied than European development. I will prepare a lesson for the next few days, and we shall discover and compare these two collective cultures." Mr. Antoine droned on but Amira, remembering her mother's advice, sat taller and appeared more relaxed than she felt. It was time to throw shade back at Gudrun. Gudrun was now invisible. No longer would Amira acknowledge the tall girl's insults. Amira would adopt her mother's way of being and for spite, just a bit of Aunt Fazha's royal bearing. Hah!

The lesson ended and Mr. Antoine went to search for his attendance and syllabus book while the students remained in their seats. Amira focused on the buzzing from a suspended light fixture. The school was old and many parts of it were literally antique. Still, she liked it here and was privileged to attend thanks to her mother's sacrifices. Some giggling started and for a brief second Amira was tempted to see what was causing it but did not. She forced herself to let her eyes roam slowly around the semi-dark room even as the giggling grew louder.

***

The lesson with Mr. Antoine continued the next day with a broadened scope for the class to consider. The students had taken their usual seats with Amira and Gudrun seated at opposite ends of the huge dark oak table. This meant the two young women often caught each other's eye and was very unpleasant.

"To continue today, we will look at one of the most conflicted, violent, and acrimonious interactions of Europe and Africa, particularly, the Congo."

"Congo," snorted Gudrun. "It sounds just like what you'd call apes, right?" Gudrun searched for *complicit* faces among the other students. "I mean, really, who names their country Congo? It isn't as beautiful as Italy, France, and Belgium. Those countries have beautiful names and elegant languages, right, Amira?" What language is spoken in Egypt, Mr. Antoine? Tell us."

"We have a young Egyptian woman seated here today, right Amira? What is the language your family speaks?" Mr. Antoine waited for her answer.

"We speak French in my family, Mr. Antoine. It is spoken in many universities and businesses, as well as English. The basic language of business among the trades people is Arabic, but there are many other dialects. Each generation adapts to the current language or primary dialect" reported Amira.

"They don't even have their own language," Gudrun *mused viciously.*

"What Amira is talking about is the *lingua franca* or the language of doing business of a particular trading system existing for millennia. People from all over the world would add new words and dialects when they traded and traveled. Governments would at times declare that a certain language, usually a preeminent one, would become the official language. Unlike Americans who rarely speak a second language, the people of Egypt and North Africa would have to speak several languages in their everyday life. This both promotes solidarity and supports diversity. People would become loyal to other cultures by immersing themselves fully in trading and social interaction" guided Mr. Antoine.

"Now this diversity and support did not extend to the colonial rule of the Congo by the King of the Belgians. King Leopold II took the Congo as his personal asset. Under his management the Congo became a place of horror and inhumanity. Many people suffered for his selfish intentions, and it took the rest of the world a bit of time to find this out. It is a horrible time in African history and many Belgians continue to apologize a century later" Mr. Antoine concluded.

"Gudrun, aren't you and your family Belgian," probed Amira seriously. "How do you feel about this horror and what your old king did?"

Gudrun looked at Amira with hate in her eyes. Gudrun was very proud of her family in the *Diplomatic Corp,* and she knew little except the sanitized history of Belgium. Then she mouthed the evil word, the n-word, at Amira. Amira pretended not to notice.

"Mr. Antoine, I would very much like to hear more about colonial atrocities especially as it affects my country and the continent. Thank you for opening my eyes," said Amira as she ignored Gudrun.

"Well, I am very happy to address any subject the students are seriously interested in. It is my joy to provide answers to your questions. Normally, you are all so bored, but I sense this subject has really connected with you today. Yes, excellent. We shall explore the Renaissance and African cultures as a counterpoint. Much more interesting. Thank you, Amira for suggesting this approach. You have a sharp mind." Mr. Antoine loaded with books and articles on the subject continued the day's lecture with new *fervor* and energy."

On the way out after class, Gudrun caught up to Amira. She spat her words at Amira.

"You're too poor to be here. You should go back where you came from." And then she used the N-word again. Several other students heard her this time and spoke to their parents about it later in the evening.

Monti is a Champ

Mr. Robinson had changed their schedule all around and this only made Monti and Amira happier. When she arrived back at their apartment after school, Mr. Robby, the doorman, would tell Amira whether Monti was in the park or at home. Some days, Mr. Robinson and Monti spent the whole afternoon walking and riding *respectively*, around the near streets in Monti's special wheelchair meeting his neighbors.

Mr. Robinson was encouraging Monti to say hello to others as he passed. When Monti said hello, it rarely sounded like hello, so Mr. Robinson would tell the *passerby* what Monti meant. This *effusive* barking noise from Monti startled people used to looking away from a sight such as Monti but often, they did say hello in return. This cheered Monti and Amira and some of the people were possibly kinder people after this encounter. They did seem to smile as they walked on, she *observed*.

Alianna was cheered by Monti's awareness of other people and his growing affection for Mrs. May and Mr. Robinson. He was excited to see each one come and go, though now Monti was much quieter on the weekends when only she and Amira were on duty. Alianna was more relaxed in her thinking and after finding her own old books she had written in Egypt during and after university, began to think about writing about her own Monti. It would give her focus and leave something for other parents working with their own children suffering as Monti was. It was worthwhile she decided and mentioned it to her ex-husband in their weekly call.

Stanley Fletcher was unsurprisingly less supportive than Alianna would have liked. He felt advertising their son's limitations would only engage pity in the readers. Besides, how would she write about Monti's father? How would she explain why and how he had left them?

Amira remembered the night her father had left for good. He had only one suitcase, and Alianna, normally calm and unperturbed, was begging him to stay, between breathless sobs. Amira had watched from behind the door of her old bedroom. Her old bedroom had looked out onto a real street, with trees, people, and cars. It was a lovely big apartment and Amira and Monti had their own rooms and bathrooms. It was a nicer place just a block away from where they now lived. Her father had promised if they let him go free, he would give them everything they needed. He promised he would always provide generously for them. He just couldn't stay with "that." He used his chin to point towards Monti's room. Amira and her mother never forgot this moment.

Amira knew, though Alianna did not suspect she did, that Stanley's promise to care for them would *peter out*. As his independent life: girlfriends, travels, and a penthouse apartment began to add up financially, the three of them began a downward thumping. Not quite a *downward spiral* Alianna and Amira both thought. It wasn't smooth after all. Their *downward trajectory* was in chunks, lumps, and bumps.

Stanley found a new apartment for them, smaller, with no view and only two small bedrooms. Then he cut the money he provided for food. Alianna insisted he keep the insurance and Monti's care up to date. But soon, Stanley Fletcher was beginning to lose big time in the *Stock Market* and his lifestyle drained even his own savings and investments. Alianna had had her own small accounts; she'd had no *dowry*, so marriage in Egypt had been impossible. But now, her money was gone.

151

Amira loved the idea of a book about Monti. She was quietly joyous that his story and her mother's would last a long time. Her mother told her to keep her fingers crossed. This might not please her old publishers in Egypt, and she was only superficially acquainted with one or two in New York. This would be a question for the cousins who must not know the contents of the proposed books. Alianna had already decided to work with Amira to write a sister's perspective for young children. And there might be some money for mother and daughter in the telling of theirs and Monti's stories.

The Telfords Need Help

Alex was waiting, sitting on the ornate concrete *balustrade* of the elegant townhouse next to Amira's faded building. He had requested, no pleaded, for Amira to come down. He planned on a walk in the park with her to talk about his plans. Amira, of course complied, and running down the stairs pulling her heavier coat on, thought she knew what this was about. She didn't know everything yet.

Alex guided her down the street and across Fifth Avenue to the park entrance. Passing under the ornate gates always open, he was silent. Amira was patient and let him find his own timing.

"He doesn't love me anymore. He wants me out of his life like we've never known each other. First, he moves out of our room, leaving all the stuff we collected on the shelves. His new room has posters and a sofa for HIS friends to hang out. He took the stereo, I don't care, but he didn't ask me for it. He walks by me in the halls at school and home as if he can't see me. He's my brother and we've spent every minute of our lives together. He doesn't even answer my questions and I wait outside his room all the time. What did I do wrong?" Alex's quiet tears ran down his cheeks, the thin shoulders of his tall frame hunched over together. He dragged his feet in the shriveled leaves, and they echoed his sad words in their own gloomy language.

The twins were the skinny tall blonde almost identical brothers in their school. They'd always dressed alike and were by each other's side throughout the day. At night, they'd talk quietly from their adjoining twin beds, and at times, when these conversations were quite heated, one or the other would lie on the carpet between to keep their voices low. They'd been happy with each other even when they fought, challenging the other to be the best. Now Axle wanted no part of their arrangement. Alex was everywhere, all the time around him, finishing his sentences and knowing exactly what he would say. Axle no longer wanted to be known for being a twin, having his thoughts guessed at, and sharing each experience.

Alex was brokenhearted. His best friend, his brother, had declared him *non persona*, a nothing, not worthwhile, inadequate, and parasitic. He couldn't take it anymore. As he and Amira walked around The Reservoir and the sky darkened, Alex began to lay out his plan. First, he demanded Amira tell no one. And she agreed not knowing yet what he planned. As Alex continued, she knew now she'd have to do something, tell someone, or intervene. This was far worse than expected and Alex, brilliant boy that he was, had everything planned out, including Amira's part in this deadly venture.

153

Why We Must Change

"Axel, come down here by the back stairs. I'll wait at the corner. Alex is on his way up in the elevator. NO! You come down here now. This is crazy stuff, and we must stop it. Yes, now. Get out the door before he sees you. Axel, this is no joke. (pause) Thank you." Amira put the house phone back into its cradle and stepped outside again to wait. She knew the Telford's building well.

The Telford's building was still huge full floor flats filled with rich families and successful young couples. The elevator opened directly into each large apartment containing several balconies throughout the apartment . It was necessary for Axel come down the back stairs. She was glad he was alone, and he would certainly do as she asked. This had gone too far. Amira had to help Axel understand what he was doing, in fact, overdoing was really harming his brother. It's true, Alex could really be a happy stalker when he had purpose but there had to be a better way. Alex's plan had made Amira, angry, sad, and desperate.

***

Aunt Fazha and Uncle Mirten spent much of their private time separately. They had their own hobbies and schedules. It was only breakfast and parties bringing them together now. Their children, Yoyo and Belem, were grown with university long behind them, good careers taking them all over the world, and their own children to care for. This left Fahza and Mirten to rebuild their lives as they wished. They had met the family dynasty's requirements, paid their social duties as needed, and now what? Even their grandchildren were happier without a granny or a nanny to surround them with love, kisses, and the giggles of long-ago babies.

Fahza could not believe how much she missed the company of young children. Mirten meanwhile, was happy to be a distant grandfather, though he spoke to his children every day from around the world. He was still building family connections including Presidents, Kings, and Generals.

Fahza was happier when she was surrounded by people. Their life in Washington DC was filled with parties and meetings but for her, the weekend was deadly dull. Egypt was much better, and they could travel for a day or two to *Monte Carlo*, and *St. Jean Cap Ferret*. Yes, that was the life Fahza wanted again but her husband was in great demand here in the American capitol. It could be years before they left. This depressed her more and more. Was this the end of her vibrant and vital family life?

She began to plan another trip back to Paris. She had many nephews and nieces there and when she got bored, she could go to London and mingle with her good friends. Truly, she lived the life of a Duchess, but what is the good if you lack a purpose for each day?

Yes, yes, go away from the darkness. Maybe she would see her *couturiers* in Paris. New clothes. This is exactly what she needed now to fill her day. Lunch with friends and nights at the casinos. Her husband's secretary would make the arrangements and Fahza started to pull some things from her closet for her maid to pack. Maybe she would cheer up. Maybe not. Then, she'd spend tomorrow and the next day in bed, curtains closed, and an uneaten lunch on a tray.

***

Mrs. May was just coming on her nightshift at the Fletcher's small apartment. She placed her dinner in the fridge, next to all of Monti's bottles, and the vegetable box the Fletchers got each week. Not a single piece of meat in their house except for her dinner. How do people live like this? All the money in the world, they could be eating steak every night, and they chose wrinkled old vegetables with dirt still on them. "People are crazy sometimes," she giggled to herself.

Mr. Robinson had had Monti out to the park again today and would again if it wasn't too cold and didn't rain. The boy was sleeping regularly now. His coughing spells were short, and his fevers had stopped. Mrs. May would turn him several times each night, gently knocking first on Alianna's and Amira's door to get some help. One or both would sleepily pad into Monti's room, and they would push and shove Monti gently, stroking his arm or leg when disturbed, until he was in a new pose. Some nights he would murmur Dingdong or Puddin, but it was back to a deep sleep for him. This was new and everyone noticed the improvement it made in Monti's day and *disposition*.

Mrs. May enjoyed being with this family. These were good people, and it was sad the distant, tense father would call but never show up for his son. Her own days were spent arguing with her *brood*, but her family was robust, energetic, and loving. This was something else. Would it go on for decades or would Monti pass from a chest infection or a heart attack? It would surely change the young girl's life. She might become bitter or even tougher than she was now. Well, Amira pretended to be tough. Cracks showed in her behavior and mood sometimes. This might get better, but it would never be perfect.

***

Amira told Axle what Alex had shared with her earlier in the park. Axel was shocked and asked Amira to tell him again. "But when," he asked Amira. She didn't know but Alex had told her he had some unfinished things, and it might take some time. How long? How long would it take to arrange these things?" asked Amira.

The two walked around the block as Axel tried to explain why he was sometimes so awful to his brother. With Monti's condition it was difficult for Amira to understand. She'd want Monti around all the time if she could. Axel countered angrily Amira certainly "would not." A constant companion gave Axel no room to change and grow. Every time Axel started something Alex had to jump in and finish it. Axel was suffocating and if he could not have his own space, at least sometimes, he might be the one who spoke to Amira, their wonderful friend, in the park. No one's life is perfect," Axel said.

"Then why not give your brother some time? Part of a day every few days. Set rules, get him to develop his own habits? He might learn to like it Axel, I know you love him, but he is hurting far worse than you are. You've had time to plan this, and he's been given no other options with no time to figure it out. Please, try to talk to him. You don't have to let him know we spoke tonight unless it's necessary and then by all means go to your parents. But please, let him back in. I'd do it for you but I'm a poor substitute. Talk. Be the good brother again but on your terms." Amira begged Axel, holding his hand tightly. Pleading with him, she did not see Gudrun and Gudrun's parents ride by in a limousine with small flags waving over the head lights.

Walking Axel back to his building, Amira gave him a big, long hug at the entrance. "I guess we have to look out for each other, Axel. This includes Alex but I think you know what I mean. Be kind to him like you always are to me.' He bent slightly and kissed her cheek. She smiled back and with a silly face pushed the tall, red-faced, reluctant boy towards the door to his building. He waved and waving merrily back, Amira headed towards her own home.

A few seconds later, there was a thud as something dropped from above, hitting the sidewalk. The next morning the building's super would pull some marvelous painted pictures from the broken cardboard box. These are good he thought. He'd tape them up on the basement walls to enjoy.

After saying goodbye to Amira, Axel entered his family's large apartment, pulling his coat off, he walked slowly to the boys' old room. He knocked gently. "Alex, buddy, I miss you. Come on and let's talk. May I come in?"

***

Early the next morning, Alianna called her Aunt Fazha to inquire about publishers she might know, for her book, or series of books. The maid said her aunt had planned a trip, but this morning changed her mind and stayed in bed. Alianna asked the maid to tell her aunt, how she and the kids missed her. They'd all love to talk to her later if she were up for it. The young maid said it would be good for her aunt to receive this message.

A Surprise Visit

Mr. Robby, the doorman, appeared concerned to Amira. They both watched the massive gray *Rolls Royce* pulling away from the curb in front of Amira's building. Amira had just walked up to see the departure herself.

"Miss Amira, there's a woman upstairs at your place. She had tons of expensive luggage, a fur coat, and it took both Vito and Toni, to get it upstairs. *Her Royal Highness* told me her cousin in Beekman Place had no room for her. You should go up. Your mom only got upstairs a minute behind her. Let me know if you need anything, okay?" Mr. Robby tipped his hat and opened the door wide, to allow Amira to pass upstairs.

The door to their small corner apartment stood open. When Amira stepped inside, she immediately saw a dozen suitcases filling up their small living room and an enormous black *sable coat* covering most of their worn loveseat. This was very interesting.

Amira tiptoed towards Monti's room where her mother stood leaning against the doorway, her hand to her mouth to cover her crying. Amira joined her at the door, slipping her long arm around her mother's slender waist. She was amazed at what she saw.

Aunt Fazha, in her perfect black dress, perfect black leather shoes, and splendid white hair, was curled up next to Monti in his bed. One long arm was draped over Monti's stomach. The other coiled around his head, stroking his flop of brown hair. She was singing an Egyptian lullaby, or maybe it was a love song, into Monti's ear. Hard to hear the words but she sang in a deep foreign whisper mesmerizing Monti into calm. His eyes wandered the room though he was lying quite still. He was never this calm when new people were around or touched him in anyway. Aunt Fahza concluded the song.

"Dingdong! Dingdong! Puddin' Puddin!" Mother and sister joined their aunt and the boy, gently reclining at the foot of Monti's bed. Amira played with his toes to make him drool.

End of Amira Dingdong - Series One

Glossaries

Little Stones Who Dream of Wings – Glossary

Chapter One

Upbeat – cheerful and optimistic

Adopted - legally take (another's child) and bring it up as one's own.

Attention deficit disorder -beginning in childhood and often persisting into later life, difficulty in maintaining attention/concentration, and often accompanied by hyperactive and impulsive behavior.

Munchausen By Proxy - **mental illness and a form of child abuse.** The caretaker of a child, most often a mother, either makes up fake symptoms or causes real symptoms to make it look like the child is sick.

Schizophrenic - combination of hallucinations, delusions, and extremely disordered thinking and behavior that impairs daily functioning, and can be disabling

Introverted - a shy, quiet person.

Optimist – one who is hopeful and confident about the future.

Stoop – stairs or landing outside the entrance to a building.

Hollered – yelled (old school).

Abide - to tolerate someone or something.

Parasites – people who want to take something from other people

Exasperation - a feeling of intense irritation or annoyance.

Musings - reflection or deep thought.

Civilization - human social and cultural development

8-track player – magnetic and multi-track music player from 1960's – 1980's

161

Philosophical - showing a calm attitude toward <u>disappointments</u> or difficulties.

Televangelists - <u>preachers</u> who appears regularly on television to <u>preach</u> and appeal for funds.

Chapter Two

Eccentric - a person of <u>unconventional</u> and slightly strange views or behavior.

Acknowledging - accepting or admitting the existence of a person or their beliefs.

Difficult - a person not easy to please or satisfy.

Medical support payments - *health care coverage for age or disability.*

Potential - the capacity to become or develop into something in the future.

Unimpeded - not <u>obstructed</u>, <u>hindered</u>, or blocked.

Askew - not in a straight or level position.

Clogs - heavy leather or wooden shoes with thick wooden soles (1960-1990).

Emphatic - expressing something <u>forcibly</u> and clearly.

Determined - made a firm decision with resolve not to change it.

Disinclined – unwilling, reluctant, won't do it.

Inevitably - certain to happen.

Hysterical - uncontrolled extreme emotion.

Resolute - purposeful, determined, and unwavering.

Blubbered - sobbed <u>noisily</u> and <u>uncontrollably</u>.

Self-assured - confident in one's own abilities or character.

Akimbo - (of other <u>limbs</u>) <u>flung</u> out widely (old school).

Beige - a pale sandy yellowish-brown color.

Grimaced – making faces twisted to show disgust, disapproval, or pain.

Badgers - a heavy, meat and plant eating, night mammal of the weasel family, with a gray and black coat.
Lazed - a relaxed, lazy manner.
Rummaged - *to make a thorough search by turning over and looking through the contents.*

Stench - *an unpleasant or foul odor; stink.*

Decrepit - broken down with age : worn-out.

Inheritance - My grandmother left me *money, property, or position.*

Well-to-do - having plenty of money and possessions.

Squats - crouch or sit with one's knees bent.

Locomotion - ability to move and the act of moving from one place to another.

Sustained - continuing action for long periods without stopping.

Contrite - feeling very sorry and guilty for something bad that you have done.

Graciously Declined – kindly say no to someone.

Asphalt – black top material on roads.

Possession – something that you own or is owned by someone else.

Afflictions - something that causes pain or suffering.

Brochures – small paper ads that offer services or food for sale.

Environment – the area around you, including people, places, and things.

Melancholy – feeling sad, maybe without knowing why.

Monotone – to speak in a flat manner without tone change.

Contemplated – to think seriously about something.

Descent – going downward in a bad way.

Hypervigilant – to stare around or look for something without stopping.

Elegant – something beautiful, well-made, and possibly expensive.

Consequences – the results of our actions.

anger management – to learn to become calm without acting out.

Chapter Three

Harem Outfit – a woman's clothing from the old Middle East

contritely – to do something because you are sorry you did wrong

Immaculate – perfectly clean

Khaki – heavy, light brown clothing, like Army uniforms

Petition – to beg or ask for in a formal way

Advanced Degrees – after four years of college, a master's, or Doctor's degree

Sophistication – to be worldly and knowledgeable at a higher level

Embarrassed – to feel shamed because of something

Trans Daughter – when a boy child decides that she is really a girl

Bicentennial – the 200th year anniversary as in the US is 200 years old

Medications – doctors give these so people will feel better and not experience pain.

Decrepitude – the state of aging when the body and mind no longer work well.

Behavior – everything we do forms a set of actions.

Majorette – a cheerleader for a band or team who throws a baton.

Relented – stopped doing something or forcing someone to do something.

Chapter Four

Tentacles – the arms of an octopus

Awkward – an uncomfortable action or scene

Intrigued – very curious

Chapter Five

Relinquished – gave up

Guardians – people appointed to care for someone

Glamourous – very beautiful

Curvaceous – a beautiful body, often used for females

Sanctuary – a place of true safety

Flourished – did well

Smirked – make a snarky, funny face

Ill-kempt – poorly dressed, not showered, sloppy

Venal – looking for money by cheating

Chapter Six

Balefully – menacing look, a mean, angry look

Group therapy – several people or children who share their stories to help each other out

Inertia – no movement, a long-time rest

Chide – to scold

Literally – exactly or as accurately as it occurs.

Figuratively – creatively, sort of, not literal or exact meaning

Assertive – confident and forcefully

Seesawed – kept changing their mind back and forth

Non-judgmental – a statement without good or bad opinion

Chapter Seven

Miniscule – very small by comparison

Barker – a person at a carnival or fair who yells to attract people to it (old school)

Business license – legal document that allows someone to do business in a certain area

Ancient – long ago, may not exist anymore

Deference – to be especially polite, show great respect

Profusely – a great amount of something or a lot of talking

Credit with suppliers – people give you goods and you promise to pay later

Coveralls. – work clothes

Provocative – to get attention from someone

Dirty look – a face made when someone is angry with you

"kill the messenger." – instead of blaming the source, we blame the person who told us about something

Chapter Eight

Adamant – unshakeable in opinion

Erratic – not constant, off and on

Aviator sunglasses – popular style of sunglasses among pilots and young people 1960s – 2010s

Vetoed – with the power to stop something completely

Noticeably – different, stands out

Nonchalantly – a confident and easy manner

Chapter Nine

CPR – cardiopulmonary respiration – lifesaving procedure, mouth-to-mouth, pumping chest

Defibrillator – a powerful electric tool to restart someone's heart

Unbearable – cannot stand it

Fatigue – state of being tired

Experienced – having knowledge and practice of something

Chapter Ten

Absentmindedly – without thinking clearly or being distracted by other thoughts and events

Renny and Jupiter – Glossary

Socio-economic issues - A way of describing people based on their education, income, and type of job.

Multiple diagnoses - "the presence of more than one or multiple chronic or long-term diseases or conditions".

Newfound sexuality – discovering one is not all boy or girl in all ways

Sexually conflicted – not sure if one feels like a male or female despite being born as male or female

Philosophical – able to calmly approach the condition of a thing or thought

Erudite - having or showing great knowledge or learning.

Path of least resistance – the easiest way to do something

Banos – Spanish for bathroom

Beemers – slang for BMW's expensive cars

Bebes – Spanish term for babies

Down payment – partial payment required to buy a home and get a loan (mortgage) for the rest

Abuela's – Spanish for grandmother's

Angeleno – Spanish reference to white people or their culture

Perps – perpetrators – the one who does something, often bad behavior

Liability insurance – if something goes wrong, such as an accident to another, this will pay

Sick leave replacements – the people who step in immediately when staff are out sick

Drag performer – a man or woman, performing as the opposite, on stage in costume

Pined – wanted, longed for, missing something or someone

Grimaced -angry face

Motown – the music organization that launched Black culture and music, worldwide

Various – many of generally the same type

Stand-ins – those who fill in for others in a place or work

Bus (tables) – to clear dirty tables in a restaurant

Federales – Spanish term for the Federal government of any country

Scowled – penetrating look towards another person

Humiliating – causing someone to feel ashamed or foolish with a frowning look

Prevailing – existing now, such as thought, behavior, practice, or customs

Gestured – movement of hand or body to indicate something

Dramatically putting a spin – turning a standard response into an over the top theatrical one

Regalia – clothes of celebration, honor, and usually over decorated

Single occupancy hotels – hotels that rent by the day, week, month to one person

Lived rough – living on the street, in a car or tent, usually within a city – homeless

168

Hair's breadth – so close it's less than the thickness of a hair

Relative comfort – one that is more comfortable than another but overly so

Served with divorce papers – a husband or wife declares their intention to divorce by legal papers

Chancy – could happen, maybe not; uncertain

Perceived – what someone thought they saw; their unique view of something

Privilege – to have more than others

Park and rec – communities have organizations that run park maintenance and activities

Young people's evolution – as young people grow, they develop their own perspective

Confounded – left speechless; unable to argue

Stripped cars – stolen cars that are broken down for the sale of the parts

Payphone – (old school) before smart phones; phones on street corners that took coins to make a call

Maneuvered – moving something or someone with a purpose in mind

Alternating – on and off, changing back and forth

Desperation – obsessed with making something happen

Bawl – (old school) to cry loudly and messily

Dolefully – expressing sorrow and sadness

Benignly – gentle way of being and acting

Darting – rushing in different directions often quickly

$100 Franklins – slang for $100 bills that have the face of Benjamin Franklin on them

Figuratively – creatively, sort of, not literal or exact meaning

Mouthed – speaking and moving lips without sound

Condescending – behaving and pretending to be better than someone else

Inner and Outer Voice – what is said versus what one only thinks

Cognitive behavioral – thinking and action, which can be different

Mindful – thinking about only one thing

"An eye for an eye" – (old school saying) means: if you hurt me, I will hurt you in the same way

Middle eastern bazaar – open air food and clothing markets that still exist all over the world

Promenade – to walk about in public to be noticed

Estados Unidos – Spanish for United States

Probability – the chance that something might happen

"Under the radar" – to go about your business without attracting attention

Momentarily – in a short amount of time

Benz – slang for Mercedes Benz, an expensive car

Transport – to move something from one place to another

Well-advisedly – it's good advice or suggestion

Blighted – destroyed or damaged by external force

Relentless aggression – unstoppable hurt and damage on something or someone

Magnitude greater – a huge increase, not something small

Reclaim – to take back from another

Nonplussed – not upset or angry, but disconcerted , surprised

Resorting – responding to something with action

Inadvertently – to do by mistake

170

Emotional blackmail – make someone feel guilty so they will do want you want

Caring to a fault – someone who cares so much it ends up hurting them

Sign of the cross – a religious action moving finger tops across the chest and body in prayer

Acknowledge – to accept or see

Retarded – abusive term for someone with challenges or a disability

Miffed – mildly angry

Immaculate – totally cleaned and well presented

Pointedly – emphasizing something over other points or similar objects

Took stock – to survey, understand, and count up

Pantomime – to use hands, face, and body to perform without speaking

Objectionable – something that cannot be accepted by people

Aping – to copy or mimic

Formulate – strategize, create, and put together

Surreptitiously – to do something to avoid being noticed

Essential – an important component to a larger group or body

Queried – asked in some detail, questioned

Deftly – expertly and perfectly moving something

Temple – the side of the face in front of the ears

Amira Ding Dong – Glossary

Self-absorption – to think only about oneself

171

Subdivided – large apartments get broken down into smaller units to keep rents lower

Ornery – difficult to be with, cranky

Introvert – someone who needs time alone to rebuild their own resources

Severely autistic – a brain defect that limits abilities and skills, making movement difficult but often advancing brain focus

Portends – a moment that signals something big and/or negative may happen

Mademoiselle – French formal for Miss, as in Miss Daisy

Ebony – a deep black color or material

Prominently – famous or projecting out from a structure

Ravishing – incredibly beautiful

Chiseled – clean cut facial lines along the jaw and cheekbones, considered beautiful

Imperceptibly – such a small movement you may not see it

Complied – agreed with and cooperated with

Deferentially – respectfully treating someone of high rank

Beekman Place – an exclusive and expensive neighborhood in NYC

Business coalition – groups of businesses gather to get their needs met, power in numbers

Extravagant – extreme spending on something

Tres fatigue – French for very tired

Distant – no speaking or listening but still in company

Cashmere – expensive and rare wool from which garments are made

Borderline – almost there, not quite angry but almost

Maitre'd – the person who runs the dining room in expensive restaurants

172

Immediately – right now, no hesitation

Cocktail – a mixture of alcohol and mixers such as water or juice

Nevertheless – objections do not matter

Disdain – to loath but not completely hate

Vulnerability disabilities – due to physical problems, people may be more sensitive to everyday issues or conditions

Not present – implies, they are physically here but their mind and soul are elsewhere

Deflated – to sink down bodily in defeat or tiredness

Context – the situation that clearly defines the moment or conflict when something happens

Defibrillator – electric medical tool, involving two handheld paddles that shocks a human heart back into rhythm

Restraints – materials or tools used to tie one's hands, arms, or legs down.

Torso cage – a medieval metal cage that pulls a human body into a certain position

Slight – an insult to another

Lilting – a musical quality to a voice or song. Sounds like singing

Knowledgeable – understands a subject in its entirety with clarity.

Composure – the way we hold our face and bodies during arguments and peaceful times.

Amenable – willing to go along and cooperate.

Acknowledgment – accepting as so, or the existence of something.

Fermenting – in humans, obsessing about a subject or person for a long time without release

Loathe – to strongly dislike

173

Struck first – to hit first, believed to be the best defense with more impact

Contentious – something that is easily argued about

Provoked – to be pushed verbally or physically into a conflict

Antiquated – something out of date, old school

Central Park – the major park in the center of Manhattan

Patrician – an aristocrat or noble person

Phonetically – to speak based on what one hears rather than what is written

Mon Cheri – French for My Dearest

Mamam – French for Mother

Deferred -to accept what others want or say even if opinions are different

Relentless – to keep at something constantly without stopping

Je t'aime – French for I Love YOU

Lacquered – A high shine, black liquid applied to wood

Double kisses – to kiss both cheeks of the other person

Tres formidable – French for Very Powerful

Gentile – to be especially well behaved and gracious

Prowess – to be very good at something

Straightaway – to do something right now

Solicitous – inquiring about your health and well-being, kind

Superstitiously – to believe in old style ways and customs

Renaissance – the years when the European and Russian countries elevated art, science, writing and music.

Passionate teacher – a teacher who believes deeply in the subject they teach

Non, non – French for No, No

Complicit – collaborate in something usually negative

Mused viciously – to speak vaguely but with hateful words

Lingua franca – the Language of Money, differs around the world based on the necessity of trading

Diplomatic Corp – the group of foreign diplomats residing within each country, representing the interest of their own country in talks and trade

Fervor – intense and passionate feeling

Respectively – to assign values in the order they are mentioned

Passerby – a stranger walking by

Effusive – offering thanks in a gushing intense manner

Observed – something that is watched or celebrated for its importance

Peter Out – energy drains out or event comes to a quiet end

Downward Trajectory – the pathway of activities or health that decline as a situation gets worse

Stock Market – usually the New York Stock Market where company shares of ownership are traded daily by brokers

Dowry – the money a bride's family puts up to entice a groom and his family

Balustrade – an iron fence that separates or protects one from falling

Non persona – a person who really exists but is ignored or kept out by others

Monte Carlo – an elegant city in the south of France based on gambling

St. jean Cap Ferret – a beautiful exclusive seaside town in the south of France

Couturiers – clothes makers who produce very expensive garments

Disposition – the way one feels most of the time, you have a sunny disposition

175

Brood – think deeply about something that makes one unhappy

Rolls Royce – a very expensive "limited for sale" car

www.ingramcontent.com/pod-product-compliance
Lightning Source LLC
Chambersburg PA
CBHW060223180626
46813CB00007B/2942